MAD DOG

MAD DOG

Nowhere, USA Book Two

NINIE HAMMON

STEREING & STONE

Chapter One

Judd Perkins was a level-headed man. Literally. Well, flat-headed anyway. Maybe it was because his mama left him lying on his back for too long when he was a baby. That's what folks said caused a kid to have a head that was flat in the back. Judd's was and maybe that was why. It suited him, though, built solid as an anvil like he was — thick and broad, with arms like sides of beef. His late wife sometimes had to work a seamstress's magic to get shirts to fit around his broad shoulders. If he'd been a tall man, he'd have been a giant. At five feet ten inches, he just looked like — what was it Julie Ann called him? — a refrigerator with legs.

And level-headed people didn't get all upset over nothing. Which was what Judd was afraid he was doing, getting all bent out of shape over something didn't mean a hill of beans.

But what if it did?

Judd had lost his pickup truck on J-Day, had been on his way to load up two rolls of baling wire from a fella in Drayton County, crossed the county line and *boom!* Wound up in the Middle of Nowhere sicker than he had ever been in his life. So sick he was heaving and praying to die at the same time, with a needle buried so deep in his skull that he still found himself walking around careful so he wouldn't dislodge it, and that'd been almost two weeks ago. He had an old farm truck, a 1961 International Harvester that wouldn't go into fourth or fifth gears because the transmission was shot, but it had a full tank of gas and would get him from Point A to Point B when the need arose. So he could take Buster in to see E.J. — Dr. E.J. Hamilton, the veterinarian — if he had to. He just didn't know yet if he had to.

He took off his John Deere cap and wiped his forehead with the back of his hand, squinting up into the woods where the dog had run off to. Just run off. That wasn't like Buster. Taken all by itself it wasn't no thang. But with everything else.

Squinting, he thought he could see the white fur of the big dog in the shadows of the trees on the edge of the woods, but he couldn't be sure. He opened his mouth to call out, "C'mere, Buster!" but he didn't. Maybe he'd ought to talk to E.J. first.

"Either crap or get off the pot," he said aloud, would have said it to Buster, who'd have wagged his tail and cocked his head to the side like he understood every word. "Either call the vet or no, ain't no sense in stewing over it all day."

He had a lot to get done today, and he found it hard to concentrate, his mind wandering off to that thing wrapped around the county that you couldn't cross, in or out.

It'd been there for two weeks now. And even the likes of Judd Perkins was … scared. He knew he wasn't the only one'd started thinking ahead, wondering how … if it didn't go away soon, how … *everything?* He'd never stopped before to consider how systems worked, how loaves of bread got on the shelves and what you could buy with a dollar, and where them big tanker trucks that showed up at the filling stations got the gasoline they pumped into them underground tanks.

He didn't know how any of that stuff worked, but figured it was all gonna stop working pretty soon and where did that leave him and his family? Wasn't nobody but his daughter, Doreen, and her girls Julie and Michelle here in the county.

The nine-year-old was taking the Jabberwock thing harder than her older sister. Michelle'd been taking piano lessons and turned out she was real good, and was on some kind of team, soccer or something. At twelve, Julie was preoccupied with rock music and the group of neighborhood girls she ran with, who, the best Judd could tell, would have snared gold medals on the Olympic giggling team.

But Michelle ... the scariness of it. 'Course everybody was taking it hard, but the kids was the ones with the wildest imaginations. He'd heard some of the stories they'd cooked up — about extraterrestrials like E.T. except with acid for blood and two sets of teeth. Or zombies. In the beginning, the first few days, Judd just wanted it to hurry up and get over with so folks could go on with life. That wacky storm had blown something in here — somehow. He'd been sure eggheads would spend years trying to figure out what it had been. Whatever it was, there would come along another storm to blow it back out in a day or two.

Only that didn't happen. Day after day, that didn't happen. Now, whenever Judd let himself think about it too long, that big vein on his temple would commence to throbbing and he imagined he could feel again that needle inside his skull.

His Mildred had been gone for going on eighteen months now, so it was just him and Buster. Doreen's lowlife ex-husband was out there in the wide world somewhere. Doing something. Doreen was doing nothing, sitting home because she couldn't go to work in Carlisle at the bank where she was a loan officer. So how was she gonna get paid? And what good did "paid" do?

He was gonna talk to her about moving back into the old house with him instead of staying in their little house on Coal Run Road in Pine Bluff Hollow. Wasn't no sense in that. Whatever was coming, he wanted them close so he could look after them. He could hunt. Woods was full of game and wasn't a better shot in the whole county than Judd Perkins. He had a garden. They wouldn't starve. But the rest of it. He just flat out didn't know.

Buster'd been acting weird for the past few days and Judd'd had too much on his mind to pay it any attention. But this morning the dog had killed a chicken. Just killed it. The chicken was out pecking at whatever it was chickens pecked at in the yard, and the next thing you know, Buster's leapt up and killed it, snapped its neck and slung his head back and forth with the chicken's body in his mouth, feathers going every which way. He'd dropped it then and walked away from the body lying there in the dirt. He was walking funny, too.

If there was something wrong with Buster … Judd didn't know how to think about that. He loved Buster like he was a kid, had hugged that dog to his chest and cried into his fur when Mildred passed and wasn't no human he woulda done that with.

Buster'd been a beautiful dog when Mildred was alive to care for that long coat of his, brushed it two or three times a week. She had taught that dog all kinds of things, got a book about training a guard dog and talked to E.J. about how you was supposed to use commands in German so couldn't nobody else control your dog. White as a polar bear, the dog was. A Great Pyrenees, he probably weighed 170 pounds, with a big, square head and eyes that followed Judd's every movement, wide, intelligent eyes that you could look into and ... sometimes Judd thought that dog could read his mind.

Buster wouldn't look at him this morning, though. He'd put the dog's food out, set the bowl on the floor and Buster wasn't interested. Judd cast a glance up into the woods at the white spot lying in the shade of that sycamore tree ... what was the dog doing up there?

Then he turned on his heel and marched into the house to the phone.

E.J.'s receptionist, Raylynn Bennett, answered, "Healthy Pets Animal Clinic, may I help you?"

Judd swallowed. "I need to talk to E.J. Something's wrong with Buster."

Chapter Two

Harry Tungate wondered how long the gasoline would hold out. Not long, he wouldn't think, and then what was everybody supposed to do? As he bounced down into the potholes in Rooster Run Road on the way to Abner's place, he was running over in his mind all the consequences of being stuck here in Nowhere County. Couldn't nobody get out. Couldn't nobody get in, neither, and he wasn't sure which was worse.

The Jabberwock.

He didn't know how it'd got named that — somebody said it'd been Holmes Fischer, the county's token homeless person, who'd come up with it and if it had been, Harry wasn't surprised it was weird. He'd always thought Fish was half a bubble off of plumb, even before he started soaking his brain in booze. That's the kinda thing Fish woulda said.

A hound-faced man with a bulbous nose that didn't have nothing to do with drinking, Harry had droopy eyes that made him look sad, or sleepy or slow on the uptake, and he was none of those things. His hair was the color of a ten-penny nail and it was getting real thin, but his twin brother Roscoe had lost even more hair — right in the center of the top of his head in the back. You could see pink showing through there like he was an antique car that'd got a bad paint job. The men had identical round bellies hanging out over their belts. But what didn't nobody know except Harry's late wife, Beatrice — God rest her soul — was that Harry had a tattoo on his belly right above his belly button. It was an eyeball. Just an eyeball. He'd been drunk when he'd gotten it, so he wasn't sure anymore why he'd thought it was a good idea, but he did remember it had something to do with the eyeball looking like his naval, or maybe it'd been the other way around. He was grateful that his mat of turning-gray chest hair come down far enough on his belly to hide the danged tattoo so you couldn't see it if you didn't know it was there.

Glancing down at the fuel gauge on his old truck again, he shook his head in dismay. A quarter of a tank. Now how in the Sam Hill was he supposed to get back and forth to town once the tank ran dry? Ride a horse? He *had* a horse, which made him a sight better off than most — along with a farm full of other animals. But wasn't no way he could use old Buttercup as a means of transportation!

They'd better get this Jabberwock thing fixed soon or everybody in the county was gonna be in a world of hurt *for real* — not just panicked Chicken Littles scared the sky was falling. Not surprising folks went a little crazy for the first week or so, saying it was an alien invasion or a zombie apocalypse or the government was testing something that went haywire or the time of tribulation had started for the return of the messiah. Things like that. Willard Crump's wife, Ethel, had run down to the root cellar and hid soon's she heard people was vanishing and then reappearing, crying and hollering and carrying on, wouldn't come out for nothing. Far as Harry knew, she was still down there. Billy Dan Singleton took his souped up, NASCAR-wannabe Chevy and was doing almost a hundred miles an hour when he crossed the county line and hit the mirage — spent the rest of the day puking blood out his nose in the Middle of Nowhere, his fancy car gone wherever all the other vehicles had gone.

Harry thought maybe it was toilet paper that finally got folks focused on reality instead of wacky stuff. Hadn't been for Viola Tackett, wouldn't have been a roll of it for sale anywhere in the county by sundown on the day after J-Day. His brother Roscoe'd been there and told him all about it.

~

VIOLA HAD honorable intentions when she went to Foodtown in Persimmon Ridge the day after the Jabber-wock sunk its sharp teeth into Nowhere County. She needed groceries, same's everybody else. Oh, she had plans for that store, for all the stores in the county, just wasn't ready quite yet to pull the trigger on them.

But when she got to the store, the parking lot was full and first thing she seen was Truman Haggardy come out to his truck and start loading toilet paper into the back of it. Them big, mega packages with three dozen rolls each. He had his whole basket full of them, enough toilet paper to wipe his butt until the Second Coming.

Mary Ellen Sweeney come out after him with her cart loaded with canned goods, all the way up to the top, and her oldest, Sue Ann, was right behind her with another cart loaded just as high. The ones quickest on the uptake had figured out they'd better get theirs before the shelves was bare, which would mean the whole county'd have to walk around with crap in their shorts before long because Tru'd bought up all the toilet paper.

That wasn't at all neighborly of Mr. Haggardy. He'd ought to thought about his fellow man before he done a thing like that and Viola intended to remind him of what the good book said about loving your neighbor.

"Neb, you go get that toilet paper out of Tru's truck and take it back in the store. Obie, you get them cans from Mary Ellen. Zach, you come with me. I'm going to have me a little talk with Oscar."

Them folks squawked like stepped-on hens when the boys started doing what she said, yelling about how they'd paid for it, didn't steal it, it belonged to them. But every mother's child in the county knew better than to cross a Tackett.

Viola'd marched into the store and seen a line of people waiting to be checked out, carts loaded to overflowing. She stood at the front of the store, not saying nothing, just motioned for the bag boy and told him to go get Oscar Manning, who owned the store. Oscar come running like a lap dog. He was one of them men who went ahead and shaved his head when he started losing his hair because he thought bald looked better. It didn't.

"You just gonna let them do that, hoard up stuff like that?"

"They ain't looting," he said. "They're paying for what they're taking."

Yeah, with money. Which was a thing too big for Viola to get her head around. What was the value of money? Maybe the value was in the fact that the folks using it thought it was valuable. And that worked, she supposed, long's folks had a reasonable supply of it. But most of the population of Nowhere County — which wasn't more than a couple thousand people, if that, she didn't care what Pete Rutherford said — was on the government dole and when them checks stopped coming, what then? They already gamed the system best as they could with liter bottles of Pepsi. Go to the grocery store the first couple of days of the month, when the checks come, and everybody you seen had carts full of Pepsi. They'd buy the Pepsi for $1.99 a bottle using Food Stamps. Then they'd wheel the carts around to the back of the building and sell the bottles back for $1.50 cash. They'd use the cash to buy whatever they wanted — used to be that was booze and cigarettes but lately that'd changed to drugs — and Oscar pocketed the difference.

Not drugs. Drug. OxyContin, and Viola had seen that one coming a long way off. She had eyes and ears everywhere and for the past couple years the free clinics in all the counties in Eastern Kentucky had seen an avalanche of people addicted to the prescription painkiller. She had herself a right good stockpile of it and now them little white pills was solid gold.

Wouldn't be long before the addicts in Nowhere County'd be looking for other ways to feed that craving. Booze and weed. She had the market cornered on them, too, and those was "renewable resources." Poor substitutes, but you'd take what you could get when you's hurting bad as them folks was gonna be hurting. She'd already been thinking about that, which looped back to money. Was money going to matter anymore? What was it folks would turn to when wasn't no money left or it wasn't worth nothing?

Could be a lotta things. Shoot, might even be something stupid as toilet paper. But whatever it was, she was gonna be first in line to secure control of it, and allowing people to hoard up stuff might be she could use later was not in her best interests.

"Now, Oscar, you ain't thought this through all the way to the end. Until that Jabberwock thing goes away, this and the Mini-Marts, 7-11's, Tuckers and the other little grocery stores is the only food available in the whole county." She nodded toward Roscoe Tungate, the butcher, who'd stopped what he was doing to come listen. Everybody in the whole store had done that. "You got the only meat there is except what's on the hoof. Ain't right to let some folks take it all, store it up for their own selves and then there ain't none for anybody else."

"They paid for it," Oscar said. "Got a right to buy however much you can carry."

"The legal right. There's legal and then there's right." She fixed him with a hostile stare. "This ain't right."

He took the hint.

"What are you suggesting? You sayin' I shouldn't sell nothing to nobody?"

"No, that ain't what I'm sayin'. I'm sayin' you hadn't ought to sell folks more'n they need." She gestured toward Truman Haggardy, who had stormed back into the store after the boys relieved him of his haul of toilet paper. "You do, and pretty soon folks is gonna have to start doing without. And folks who are doing without … well, they ain't usually in the best mood, likely to … do just about anything."

She turned to the crowd. "You good folks wasn't thinking about being neighborly when you filled up them carts but now that you been reminded how you'd ought to treat folks, you ain't gonna mind putting all that stuff back" — she paused, looked pointedly at several people in line — "are you?"

"My family's got to eat," said Ramona Mattingly.

"You can't tell me I can't buy groceries," said George Gribbins.

Before others could speak, Viola put on her game face. She nodded at Neb, Obie and Zach standing by the door.

"You want this to get ugly? I can do ugly. I don't never play for pennies. You want in this game, you better be prepared to go for broke."

Nobody spoke.

Viola stuck a smile on her face that hung there like a sheet on a clothesline.

"You get the groceries you'd have bought if there wasn't no mirage thingy hanging on the county line. You get yourselves enough to last you a few days." She turned to Oscar but spoke loud enough for everyone to hear. "And Oscar here, he ain't gonna sell you no more'n that … are you, Oscar?"

"Nope," was all he said.

"And if anybody tries to make Oscar do something unneighborly, Oscar's gonna let me know about that, and whoever does something like that will be getting a little visit shortly from my three boys."

Then she just stood there. Sometimes the best club to beat somebody over the head with was silence. One by one, the people in line turned their carts around and started back down the aisles. She watched for a few minutes, then turned to Oscar.

"You done right, Oscar," she said. "I always remember them as does right by me."

Then Viola went to the shopping carts, pulled one out of line, and started to gather up her own groceries.

Chapter Three

As he turned off Rooster Run Road onto Zebulon Pike, Harry Tungate was still thinking about toilet paper, wondering how long his two rolls was gonna hold out. Likely most other folks was doing the same calculation. When Viola'd locked down Foodtown two weeks ago, the realness of their situation had hit home with people, settled them down and focused them. Not being able to wipe your butt'd sober any man.

Being a practical sort, Harry Tungate didn't waste any mental energy trying to figure out what the Jabberwock was and why it'd happened. They was smarter people than him in the county who could figure out that part. And there was bound to be folks out on the other side of the Jabberwock who was trying to figure it out, too. The government and such. He'd bet the biggest story on *The Today Show*, *Meet the Press*, *60 Minutes*, and *Dateline* every night was about this little place in Kentucky couldn't nobody get into. He did wonder sometimes what happened to people who challenged the Jabberwock from the other side, though. Where'd they get transported to and was they sick when they got there?

He shook his head to get that thought out of his mind. He hadn't never been and praise Jesus hoped never to be again as sick as he had been that day he and Roscoe'd headed up Lexington to see what was taking Leon so long to bring them their beer. Roscoe had took a week's vacation from Foodtown starting on Monday and the two of them and some other buddies was planning on spending it fishing in the Rolling Fork. Maybe take a day and drive up to Lake Cumberland and wet a hook there. They'd needed that beer, so Roscoe'd come by and picked him up and they'd headed out …

And wound up in the Middle of Nowhere. Sick. Didn't last long but for the time it did, he thought it was gonna kill him. Like it did Abby Clayton.

That wasn't anything Harry let himself think about. He'd been there. He and Roscoe and Abner had stayed around to help out once they seen what kinda shape folks was in when they got there. He shoulda left before he seen Abby, though, would give just about everything he owned — which, granted, wasn't a whole lot — to wipe that image out of his mind. Her head … pieces of it flying ever which way. A piece of something, he didn't know what and didn't want to know, had hit his shoe and he'd scraped it off on the asphalt.

At least it was Roscoe's car and not Harry's truck that got took that day. Roscoe lived on Kelly Branch Road on the south side of Callahan Mountain — wasn't but a few miles from the Ridge. Harry lived in Soloman Hollow on the north side of the mountain, had to go all the way around it to get to town and that was a hike. Roscoe could do without a car a sight better than Harry could do without a truck. Except when the gasoline ran out, Harry wouldn't have no truck, neither.

Harry fired up a prayer — out loud. Since he lived alone, he almost always prayed out loud. Kept it clear in his mind that he really was carrying on conversation — he just couldn't hear the other side of it, that's all: "I know you's getting tired of hearing about this, God, but I'm gonna have a hard row to hoe if there ain't no gas and I can't go nowhere. I'm asking you respectful-like to fix this thing and make everything like it was before. Amen."

That was another way him and Roscoe was different. Oh, Roscoe wasn't bad as some — guys who wouldn't recognize a bigger meaning to life if God punched them in the face wearing a ring that left the initials G.O.D. on their foreheads. But Roscoe didn't believe strong as Harry did. Though what was going on now mighta made a believer outta him and a whole bunch of other folks, too.

Abner Riley, now — there was a man of faith. Harry was glad to be spending time with him today because he never left Abner without feeling better about life.

Wasn't hard to see why Abner was so spiritual. That harelip of his that his daddy'd sewed shut with a needle and thread when he was three or four years old, had been a life burden that'd either humble a man and send him to his knees — or make him bitter. Though Abner never said much — he didn't like to talk because he sounded so funny — when he talked about God you's hearing from a man who'd got up close and personal.

Harry'd told Abner he'd come over today and help him work on that Allis-Chalmers tractor that'd been sitting in Abner's shed gathering dust for probably a decade. It'd made sense to Abner — and Harry agreed — that might be a good idea to plant a garden this year even if gardening wasn't something you usually done. There was a piece of flat bottom land out behind Abner's house that he was thinking of tilling up and planting vegetables. With gasoline, once it's gone, won't be no more of it, but food was a different thing altogether. This was a farming community and folks here wasn't likely to starve to death because of the Jabberwock — though the complexities of how Nowhere County farmers' produce and beef was gonna wind up on the plates of county residences — that was another thing he'd leave up to other folks to figure out.

Roscoe'd pointed at a flock of birds flying across a field the other day and wondered if maybe the people outside who was working on getting rid of the Jabberwock might send in supplies — like them airdrops you seen on TV where the army puts stuff on airplanes and drops it at the end of a parachute to the folks who've had an earthquake or hurricane or such as that. Maybe they'd send in supplies to Nowhere County. But the thing the county needed most, in Harry's opinion, was fuel and that wasn't something you could drop out an airplane at the end of a parachute.

Abner had a little house back deep in Fearsome Hollow on Fog Bottom Lane off Gabe Stump Road, and Harry teased him about the "haints" that was his "neighbors," asked him had he ever seen one and was they scary. Everbody'd growed up hearing tales about the spirits, or ghosts — the old folks called them haints — that lived there in the mist. He supposed that's why it'd got named Fearsome Hollow, because the mists made it all spooky-like. The Smokies in Tennessee got named the Smoky Mountains for the same reason — mist, which was like to show up anywhere in the Smokies, not just in the one hollow like it done here. When you got up high in one of them overlooks in Great Smoky Mountains National Park, you'd swear the place was on fire — smoke here and there, hanging over that valley or down in that hollow or above that ridge.

Wasn't smoke, of course, just mist, and it was the same with Fearsome Hollow — the mist would be hanging over Troublesome Creek one day and the next it'd be up at the top of the hollow so thick you couldn't even see Buzzard Knob.

Didn't hardly nobody go all the way out to Abner's and that was a shame 'cause those who did was like to be surprised at what a nice place he had. Oh, wasn't big but it was red brick and Abner put another coat of white paint on the trim, the shutters and the picket fence every spring. He didn't make much as an orderly, had said once it took him five years to save up enough for a down payment, and once he got the place and fixed it up nice, he kept it so pin neat Roscoe teased him about using scissors on the grass in the front yard.

Harry didn't park in the driveway, just pulled off the road onto the shoulder in front of Abner's house and killed the engine. He hadn't even got out of the truck before he noticed that Abner's front door was standing wide open.

That was odd. He paused, sat looking at it.

It had got quiet all sudden-like, no sound but the ticking of the engine cooling off. It felt kinda spooky, though wasn't no mist. Mist made it creepy sometimes but wasn't nothing but bright blue sky and sunshine now. He opened his door and got down out of his truck and hollered for Abner, who musta been around the side of the house or something, otherwise he'd have closed the door when he walked out.

There was no answer.

"Yo, Abner, where you at?" For no reason he could explain, Harry didn't want to open the front gate and go up the walk to that open door. That was crazy.

"You born in a barn, boy?" he called out from where

he stood by the open door of his truck, but he didn't get any closer to the house. "You left your danged door open."

The only response was silence. A full, heavy, throbbing silence. There was a screen door on the back but wasn't even a storm door on the front so Abner was letting in flies and bugs and …

Harry's heart kicked into a gallop. Why, maybe Abner was sick or something, fell down and hit his head …

Why was the door open?

And why was there …? No, that was crazy, just his heebie-jeebies getting to him. He stood still, just looking, listening. And it was real — there really was a cool breeze blowing out that front door. Musta had the back door open, too — with the screen shut, of course. So there was a draft …

It was a warm June morning, probably get up into the eighties by afternoon.

Wasn't warm in that house, though. No sir. It was—

Cold as an empty grave …

When the bones are tossed away.

Harry turned around so fast he got his feet tangled up and almost fell down on his butt. But there wasn't nobody there. Well, somebody — *two somebodies* — said …

An unreasoning terror seized Harry's heart and squeezed so hard he couldn't get his breath. He leapt back into the truck, fumbled around with shaking fingers to fit the key that was still in his hand back into the ignition.

When the engine roared to life, he reached for the gearshift to put the truck in gear and the house …

It was a dream, had to be, wasn't no way a house could … *breathe.* Could inhale so the walls swelled outward. Then exhale, blow a breath of cold out the front door that rushed down the sidewalk to Harry's truck. Harry slammed the gearshift into drive with a strength that might have ripped the knob off the top of the handle. He jammed his foot down on the accelerator and yanked the steering wheel in a full-lock turn left. The old truck shuddered and spun around in the road, kicking up a plume of dust in the air behind him as he roared away.

But not before that cold hit his truck.

Not before he gasped in a breath and breathed back out … and his own breath frosted in the air in front of him.

Chapter Four

Charlie McClintock opened her eyes and the period of fuzzy unreality — that blissful non-place where you were back in an ordinary world with reasonable rules and everything was right in the universe — lasted only four or five seconds. It seemed to her that the period of unawareness before her mind reoriented was getting shorter and shorter every day. It wouldn't be long before she opened her eyes and knew instantly that she was a captive, could not leave Nowhere County, Kentucky. Knew that an invisible barrier called the Jabberwock would hurl her back to the Middle of Nowhere if she tried, and "hurl" was the right word because she wouldn't just be miraculously transported — she would be projectile vomiting when she got there. Or worse. As far as she knew, the only person who had ever ridden the Jabberwock more than one time was Abby Clayton. And she had … exploded.

Charlie paused. Waited. Looked at the ceiling of her bedroom where the shadows of tree limbs danced to the tune of the morning wind. Nope, it still wasn't there. She still could find not a shred of compassion for the woman who had locked Charlie's precious three-year-old daughter in an airless kiln. Or would have if she'd had the strength; the intent had been there. Charlie wanted to be compassionate because she saw herself as a compassionate person, a better person than she was allowing herself to be right now. Maybe someday.

Charlie had even intended to go to Abby's memorial service, had written it on the calendar on the wall in the kitchen beside her mother's big "Not in Kansas Anymore, **ToDo**" blackboard. But she hadn't gone. She couldn't go without opening the door on the memories of those nightmare hours when she thought her precious baby was dead, suffocated, murdered by Abby Clayton. And even though she never allowed herself to think about it, the memories were like a drip of black ink in a glass of water, they spread out and darkened everything. She wanted that part to be over. Going to the service would just spread more black ink.

That would be a step backward and today Charlie had planned a step forward, toward accepting the unacceptable, not about Abby and her attempted murder of Merrie, but about Charlie and *life as we know it on the planet*. This was about tomorrow and the other tomorrows stacked up on the other side of it.

She'd left Nower County the morning after she graduated from high school and hadn't returned but a couple of times in the fourteen years since. She'd started college, but hadn't made it past her freshman year courtesy of the momentous day disguised as a totally ordinary day when her English professor assigned a children's story as the class's writing assignment.

She wrote it during her breaks at the Dunkin' Donuts where she worked, turned it in, got the paper back with no grade and the words "See me after class" written in red on the top. Goody. She really needed to make an A in this class because the required math (algorithms) and science (geology) classes were kicking her butt.

Her story was good, he'd told her, really good. Like industrial-strength good — and she was glad he liked it, she really was, but if he didn't shut up about it she'd be late for work. Did she mind if he showed it to a friend of his in publishing? If he'd just give her an A and stop babbling, she didn't care if he used it to potty train a puppy.

That was eleven books in a twelve-book series ago. A bestselling fantasy for middle school-age kids that captured the imaginations of readers from eight to eighty. Hollywood made into it the most popular cartoon series on television. And the movie deal was all but sewn up. The twelfth book had pre-order sales in the ba-jillions and it wasn't even written. She knew the plot, though, and it would be the best book of them all.

Then her mother had washed overboard off a yacht in the Florida Keys, Charlie had come home and … the Jabberwock.

Writing was more to Charlie than what she *did*. It was *who* she was. This enforced sabbatical had backed words up in her mind like a clogged sewer and the pressure was building. So she'd made a decision. She'd get out of Nowhere County eventually — she believed that, *had to* believe that — and when she did, she'd have something to show for the time she'd spent incarcerated here. She would write the twelfth book, which ironically, was about an invisible dragon.

Charlie certainly had plenty of time on her hands now to write. For two weeks, she'd been struggling to fill her days. She hung out as often as she could with Sam, E.J. and Malachi, but Sam and E.J. both had jobs that still mattered in the "new normal" and Malachi lived so far out in the sticks you'd have to leave a trail of bread crumbs to find your way back. She and Sam had reconnected emotionally like they were still in fifth grade and the more Charlie came to know the woman Sam had grown to be, the more she respected her. She'd made a *life* in Nowhere County, had a Mother-Teresa-esque vibe among the most isolated nowhere people, was raising a son, a fine young man whose father was … who/where? She and Sam hadn't gotten that far yet, would eventually, though. Sam had made references to several men she'd dated over the years, but her son's father hadn't yet come up. Neither had Merrie's father.

Charlie had cleaned and polished and organized her mother's house — found paint and repainted a bedroom, even tried her hand at using her mother's sewing machine. Major fail there. Other people weren't as fortunate as Charlie, were even now having to scramble for essentials, planting gardens or making "trade agreements" with neighbors — I'll trade my five pounds of sugar for your fresh tomatoes. Sylvia Ryan hadn't been a hoarder. She'd only nudged up against the title because she'd had a huge garden and like every other woman in the county, she "canned" what she grew there. The rows of shelving that once held pottery in the garage were now weighed down, stacked three and four deep, with hundreds of Mason jars filled with garden vegetables along with jellies, jams, preserves and chutney her mother made from fresh fruit. Though the cellar was full of the flotsam and jetsam of a lifetime, there was also a huge freezer down there full of meat. The kitchen cabinets were jammed with everything from Spam to bean dip. It wasn't a magic pitcher. Eventually, Charlie's supplies would run out. Everybody's would. And then … She'd cross that bridge when "and then" got here.

There was a fly in the buttermilk of her decision to write, however. A pretty significant fly. More like a hummingbird. She didn't have a typewriter. She assumed her mother still had the old manual typewriter she'd learned to use as a teenager, which had a certain appeal. There was something about that grand physical flourish of reaching up and throwing the carriage at the end of a line that was emotionally and psychologically appealing.

She had, of course, used an electric typewriter to write her first couple of books, and hitting the return/enter key carried its own danger — no one would ever know how many cups of coffee went flying when the carriage on her electric typewriter went shooting back to the right — the ruined manuscripts, the shattered vases.

But she had searched her mother's house and couldn't find the old manual typewriter anywhere. She'd seen a typewriter in E.J.'s office she bet she could talk him out of. Then she'd found the unopened pack of ten legal pads in the closet under the stairs and thought — why not? Tennessee Williams had written every word of his glorious plays — *Cat on a Hot Tin Roof, Streetcar Named Desire* — in longhand. She recalled a quote from one of her favorite British authors, Fay Weldon, about a "mystical connection between the brain and the actual act of writing in longhand."

Charlie decided to give it a shot. If it didn't work out, she'd have a talk with E.J.

She needed an office, too, and she certainly wouldn't be using her mother's sewing room for its intended purpose. She just had to get rid of all the sewing paraphernalia, haul it up to the attic. Pens and pencils? The junk drawer in the kitchen. When she went there to start digging through it, her mother's blackboard caught her eye and she stopped digging and looked at it. It hung on the wall beside the calendar next to the refrigerator and she stepped in front of it, put out her hand and almost touched what was written in the upper left corner in chalk. *Get bird seed.* Just those three words. Her mother'd jotted them down on her ToDo blackboard … sometime.

Charlie had gotten seed. Had scattered it beneath the kitchen window where her mother liked to stand and watch the birds while she washed dishes. But she hadn't erased the words, would never erase them. They were a connection to her mother she couldn't explain. Like the blackboard opened up a portal somehow that Charlie didn't want to close.

Chapter Five

Grace Tibbits itched all over, itched in places it wasn't humanly possible to itch — like under your fingernails. It took all the willpower she had not to scratch. She didn't want Reece and the others to see her do that because they'd know what it meant. And it wouldn't do any good if she took a garden claw — and that's what she felt like doing — and raked it up and down her back. The itching wasn't *on* the skin. It was *under* the skin. And all the scratching in the world wouldn't make it any better. It'd just make her skin raw, so then the bottom side of her skin would be itching and the top side would be raw and that sounded like something that could ruin your whole day.

"You want something to drink, Mama?" Reece asked. And she knew why he was asking. She knew he was keeping track of how many times she got up to go pee. What he didn't know was she threw in another time or two here and there that weren't real, said she was going but just went into the bathroom and closed the door, stood there for a little bit, then flushed the toilet and washed her hands and came back out.

The itching was because toxins were building up in her body. Because her kidneys — little shriveled up things that they were, couldn't clean her blood. Hadn't been able to for more than two years now. She went twice a week to the hospital in Carlisle for dialysis. Well, she did back when it was possible to cross the Beaufort County line without engaging in an entertaining round of projectile vomiting in a parking lot bus shelter.

And as awful things went, projectile vomiting was about as bad—

No, it wasn't as bad as it could get. Blowing up like there was a hand grenade in your chest — that was worse.

Poor Abby Clayton. That child was dumb as a shovel but she did love that little baby something fierce and she would have done anything to get to him. Including blasting body parts and gray matter all over the Dollar Store parking lot. Grace was grateful she hadn't been there to see it happen. She had left before Abby came back that last time. And she'd told her oldest son, Reece, "The shape that poor girl was in after the second time, it's not hard to believe that one more pass and her body'd bust open like a pimple."

"Mama!" he'd said, horrified.

She did a lot of that — horrified her children. They'd decided their own selves what their mother'd ought to be — based on what she never did figure out. But it was an idealized version of motherhood, like those "Breck" girls on the outside of the hair color boxes in the 60s — all perfect. Maybe they'd got their image from hair color boxes or television or some book somewhere or just made it up in their own heads. Grace never did know, but she did know she never had come close to that image. Just for fun, she'd once put on a fake pearl necklace to do the dishes, hoping they'd get the *Leave it to Beaver* reference, but it blew right past them.

She'd asked Reece to bring her into E.J.'s clinic today to see Sam, didn't want to do their regular home visit because she wanted to talk privately with Sam. She needed somebody to be real with and if there was anybody for that job it was Sam Sheridan. And maybe she could get Sam to have a talk with Reece. He was the worst. The girls, Audrey and Mary Jo, just gave her miserable looks and thought of something they had to do in another room — like she was already dead and not just on the way. And Oliver wasn't here. He'd gone to spend the weekend with his girlfriend in Ashland — he didn't think she knew that part — so he'd missed the whole show.

She hated that. She would have liked to have had a chance to tell her youngest son goodbye.

Raylynn Bennett looked up and called out "Grace Tibbits" and Reece stood up like a jack-in-the-box, powdering sawdust off his coveralls to the floor. He was a carpenter, wearing his customary work clothes — overalls over a white tee shirt — and should have dusted off the sawdust before he came in. These days, he was too distracted to think about being polite.

"I am fully capable of doing this all by myself."

"I want to be there for you."

"You have been, and don't think I don't appreciate it. But I am seventy-nine years old and I really am ready to cross the street by myself."

"This isn't a joke, Mama."

"It is if I say it is. Goodness, boy, you get your panties in a wad every time I fart. I promise on the soul of your poor dead father" — a carousing drunk who'd bailed out on the family while the kids were still young enough to believe the tale she'd made up about him being killed at

28

sea — "that I will not drop dead between here and the examining room. I can guarantee that much. Beyond that, all bets are off."

She leaned on her cane when she walked. She hated that, but she supposed it was better than face-planting on the floor and she had gotten very weak. On J-Day, after she'd gotten her fire-hydrant nose bleed under control, she'd been strong enough to stay around and help with the "wounded." She'd been up squirting puke off the parking lot while Reece was still too sick to do anything but groan. She barely had the strength to walk now, though. Dead kidneys would do that to you.

Raylynn opened the examining room door and Sam looked up from jotting something on a chart and burst into the smile that planted a dimple in her right cheek. Why couldn't Reece have found a girl like Sam instead of that insipid little church mouse, Cissy, who was afraid of her own shadow? Of course, Sam would have been strictly off limits. More important than the fact that she was twenty years too young, she was over six feet tall. Poor Reece had topped out at five feet eight inches and that boy's ego was far too fragile to survive looking up at the woman on his arm.

"Grace! How are you?" she said in that husky voice of hers.

The veterinary clinic had been transformed into a medical facility in the two weeks since J-Day. She didn't know who exactly had done it, but if she was to guess she'd say Charlie whateverherlastnamewasnow, Liam, E.J., maybe even Malachi Tackett — which was a wonder Grace would dearly love to live long enough to see unfold. She'd glanced into the five transformed exam rooms as she hobbled down the hallway. Exam Room 1 on the end was the biggest, with several small exam tables and wire

kennels of all sizes. Double doors in the back of the room
led to the hallway of the animal hospital with "hospital"
rooms and kennels on both sides where litters of unwanted
kittens and puppies meowed and yapped alongside recov-
ering animals — a goat with a broken leg, a sheep with an
infected eye and pets in all shapes and sizes.

Sam had on the white lab coat she always wore on her
home visits. She'd confided to Grace that wearing it was
kinda playing make believe for her, pretending to be a
doctor, and now … well, she and E.J. provided the only
medical care available for the … however many people it
was who lived in the county.

That'd been discussed more in the past two weeks than
in all the seven-plus decades Grace Tibbits had lived here.
It'd suddenly seemed important to know how many people
lived in and were now *stuck in* Nowhere County. Who
knew? Until two weeks ago nobody cared.

They — whoever "they" were — had gone to consider-
able trouble to make this vet clinic a facility for humans. It
was certainly big enough, might be the only thriving
commercial concern in the whole county. E.J. had patients
in all the surrounding counties, looked after thoroughbreds
on horse farms as far away as Lexington.

But some things weren't changeable. No comfortable
examination table, just metal, more like a big tray in case a
dog-patient decided to take a leak. Grace could have tried
to haul her butt up onto the metal tray/examining table,
she supposed, but they really didn't have to worry that she
was going to pee anywhere. Peeing was a skill Grace
Tibbits was quickly losing.

"How about we cut to the chase," Grace said, and saw
the smile settle into Sam's face but not fall off. It was real.

"I'd bend over and show you but you can see for yourself. I'm starting to swell up like a toad." She didn't make

any reference to how Abby Clayton's looked when she appeared in the Middle of Nowhere that last time but they were both thinking about it. "That'd be fluid retention."

Grace ticked the symptoms off on her fingers.

"Itchiness, check. Shortness of breath, check. Fatigue — I'm so tired it makes me tired to think about being tired. Weakness. I don't know why they list that as a separate symptom because it's the same thing as fatigue. Irregular heartbeat, check. I don't yet have confusion, or if I do I'm too confused to know it. Nausea, not yet, thank you, Jesus. And ..." She paused, looked directly into Sam's blue eyes. "And the seizures, coma and death parts are, I am sure, coming soon to a kidney-free person near me."

Sam said nothing, just reached out and took her hand.

"I'm dying. I know it. You know it. My kids know it. But they refuse to accept it. What they don't get is I need them to come back to reality out of la-la land because ... I want to say goodbye. How can I do that as long as they're still pretending *everything's fine, Mama, you'll be better tomorrow, you'll see.*"

When Grace saw the tears appear in Sam's eyes and slide down her cheeks, she thought to herself: Why couldn't Reece have married Sam Sheridan?

"It's Reece I'm worried about. He gets wound tighter and tighter every day, desperate to find some way to help. I don't want to sound like a harbinger of doom, but that boy's liable to do something absolutely crazy."

Chapter Six

After determining that there were, indeed, all manner of writing instruments in the kitchen junk drawer — pens, pencils, Sharpies, Magic Markers — Charlie called out, "Merrie, where are you?"

She hated the anxiety she always heard in her voice when she called out to the child, which, of course meant the child wasn't within sight and Charlie's gut yanked into a knot whenever she couldn't look at her little girl. See her. Reach out and touch her. Even when she could hear the sounds of her playing in the next room, Charlie felt anxious and uneasy. She had paid dearly for the privilege of overprotecting her three-year-old. Still, she hoped it would ease off because it wasn't good for Merrie, or for her either. Charlie would work on it. But not today.

"Here, Mommy," piped a voice from the living room, where Merrie had spent the better part of the morning taking the cushions off all the furniture and stacking them on the floor, and trying to drape blankets over them to make a tent so she could camp out.

"Come on up into the attic with me."

"I busy."

"Get un-busy."

"I making a town."

"Good, if there's anything Nowhere County needs it's a new town, but you can finish it later."

"I don't wanna come."

Charlie bit back her response. She had to return to the mother/daughter relationship she'd had before the nightmare eternity when she'd believed the little girl was dead. This pleading, begging tone she heard in her own voice when she told the child to do something was unhealthy. Had to fix it.

"You don't have to *want to* come. But you *do* have to come." She paused for a beat. *"Now."*

The little girl emerged from the living room and the sunlight streaming through the doorway lit up her face and Charlie almost gasped from how beautiful she was. Oh sure, all mothers thought theirs were the most beautiful children who ever drew breath, but Merrie ... Her eyes were show-stoppers, blue like Charlie's, but a shade lighter — the color of a robin's egg or the sky on a summer afternoon. Set against her olive skin they were arresting, seemed to glow like blue jewels inside a fan of long, black lashes. And the shiny black curls and full lips that were her heritage from her father's side of the family ... she was gorgeous.

"I wanna play in my fort." She stuck out her lip in a pout.

"Don't you want to climb a ladder?" Taking her hand, Charlie led her into the hallway, reached up and grasped the dangling fob that pulled down the retractable folding attic stairs. She lifted Merrie to the ladder.

"We're going up into the top part of the castle, where we can look out the window and see the whole kingdom."

"An I'm a princess!" Merrie was instantly into the fantasy. Clearly, imagination was as hereditary as her beauty. "You get to be the ... the lady who milks the cows."

There was surprisingly good light in the attic, with windows at both ends on the dormer and three lights on wires with pull chains. Charlie pulled the ladder back up after her and fastened the latch so it couldn't be pulled back down, and so it wouldn't fall down if Merrie stepped on it.

The little girl ran to the window and looked out.

"I see giraffes. An elephants and koala bears — red ones."

"My, but we have an eclectic array of wildlife in our kingdom."

"They're not electric. Animals don't have plugs. They have batteries."

Merrie settled into her pretend role while Charlie considered how best to scoot what was already here around so she could bring up all things seamstress from downstairs to take its place. She had just about finished rearranging the attic contents when the box fell on her head.

It had been on the top of the chifforobe — which Charlie could only assume had been constructed in the attic because she could see no way that it could have been moved up the ladder from downstairs. It was next to the window that looked out over the backyard and the woods and mountain beyond. The dirt yard was getting green again, but Charlie didn't look out the window. She still couldn't look at the kiln without becoming almost physically sick, even after she'd gotten Lester Peetree from the hardware store to come over and remove the kiln door. It hadn't been that hard to do working from the inside where you could get to the hinges. She would have hauled the whole thing off to the dump, but there was no way to pick it up and no dump in Nowhere County. She planned to take a sledgehammer to it and beat the whole thing into little pieces of rock … *someday.*

The big piece of furniture had double doors on the front and an interior that was reminiscent of *The Lion, the Witch and the Wardrobe.* It wasn't too heavy now that it was empty. She set her back against the double doors and shoved with her legs. When she did, it tipped, and a box she didn't know was up there slid off the top and crashed down onto her head.

It could have been a box full of bricks. Okay, realistically, it really could have been full of books or pottery. It was neither. It was a cardboard box full of papers and assorted junk and when it hit her head, the top flew open, and the box vomited its contents all over the floor. She rubbed the spot on her head where the box had clocked her, then got down on her hands and knees to pick up the spilled papers.

A picture drawn in crayon. Stick figures. "I love you Mommy" and a heart.

A penmanship paper. Did kids even use those anymore? "Mallory" was printed on the top and below it were sets of three lines, where you printed a letter in lowercase, so the top of the O fit beneath the middle dotted line, and the top and bottom of the O hit the top and bottom lines. School papers and things Mama had kept. Mallory's third-grade report card. She opened it up. There was an S, which meant satisfactory, in every column. But an S- in the column "plays well with others." Even as a kid, her older sister had had issues.

"Merrie, come help me put this stuff back in the box."

"I busy."

"Do what Mommy tells you."

Was it Charlie's imagination, or was the three-year-old

determined *not* to do what she was told? Did that mean she was spoiled? No. Spoiled kids got whatever they wanted and nobody ever told them no. That wasn't a definition of Merrie's life. Okay, not spoiled, stubborn. Yeah. She sighed. You could do something about spoiled, but stubborn went all the way to the bone.

"Who's dis?"

Merrie had approached and reluctantly started picking up papers. She held out a photograph that had been in the box with them. Charlie took it, glanced at it before she dropped it in the ... Her eyes snapped back.

The picture showed three children — three gap-toothed little kids, which meant they all were six or seven years old and missing key teeth in front. Two little girls and a little boy. One of the little girls had flaming red hair. The little boy's hair was black. She settled down on the floor to study the picture, a smile of recognition growing on her face. It was a picture of her and Sam and Malachi. Where had the three of them been when the picture was taken? She didn't remember. They had wide grins on their faces and were standing in the dirt in front of a shack.

A piece of a memory fluttered through her mind and was done. An old woman with white hair and a face wrinkled like a witch. Her teeth were blackened stumps, like a forest after a fire. Her eyes were alive, though, bright, blue and fierce. Frightening. Her fingers were gnarled and lumpy, grasping Charlie's arm. Her palm was lined with deep grooves when she held out her hand. In it was a jewel.

Chapter Seven

E.J. Hamilton, *Dr. E.J. Hamilton*, stepped into the small bathroom in the corridor of the Healthy Pets Veterinary Clinic and Animal Hospital, closed the door behind him, took a deep breath, shut his eyes and tried to calm down.

This was insane. *Insane.* He was a veterinarian. A vet. He treated *animals* — dogs, cats, cows, pigs, horses, even the occasional exotic pet like the python the little Donaldson boy had. Or the iguana that got loose in the office, ran out into the waiting room and right up Dorothy Prudell's leg. Dorothy'd grabbed it and held it out to him. "Lose something?" While the one-eyed cat she'd brought in for shots hissed and spit and looked like one of those cartoon cats that were really witches' familiars.

E.J. stepped to the sink, turned on the water, cupped his hands in it and rubbed the cool water on his face. He looked at his reflection in the mirror above the sink, water dripping off his chin, and he looked every bit as stressed out as he felt. Why would anybody want him to treat their ailments — if he'd seen the look that was on his face right now on anybody else, he wouldn't have trusted that person to change the oil in his tractor.

Right now, there were three people out there in the waiting room. Not people bringing him their pets. People bringing him their infected toenails, their mysterious pain in the groin — dear Lord, what might *that* be? And Grace Tibbits, who traveled twice a week to Carlisle for dialysis because her kidneys didn't function anymore. If the Jabberwock kept the county locked up, she'd be dead inside a week. Probably sooner.

If the Jabberwock …

It wasn't an "if" for E.J. And he couldn't have said why that was or when he had come to that conclusion. It might even have been the day he'd loaded up what could not have been a more disparate assortment of humanity into his van and traveled to the county line to see it, the thing that had been hurling people into the Middle of Nowhere all that morning.

He'd stood a bit off to the side, examining the shimmer as Liam tossed a rock through it. Something clicked in his head as he studied it, snapped shut with such finality he was surprised the others hadn't heard it. His mind often worked like that, leapt out in front of his reason and came to a conclusion. It was always a conclusion his mind came to eventually, working its slow way through a labyrinth of logical sequencing. Often when he 'figured something out" he was merely acknowledging the truth his mind had already told him. This thing, this Jabberwock, wasn't going to disappear by tomorrow morning. Wouldn't be gone the next day either. Maybe not even the next. He certainly didn't know what it was or where it had come from, but he was unswervingly confident that he knew where it was going — nowhere anytime soon.

And because it wasn't, there would continue to be a

steady stream of *humans,* homo sapiens, in the lobby of his animal hospital — *animal* hospital — awaiting his care. Sure, a few basic principles applied across species. But nobody was asking him to treat a mountain lion instead of a tabby cat. They were asking him to treat a little girl who had a rash and maybe it was measles. He had no idea what a measles rash looked like. Dobermans didn't get measles.

If it hadn't been for Sam Sheridan, he'd have ... yeah, he'd have what? Run away? Sam *did* understand human anatomy, she did know about dispensing medications and all manner of other *people* things E.J. didn't. She was way more the doctor here than he was. She should have been in charge instead of E.J., who had won the captain-of-the-ship lottery by virtue of two letters in front of his name: Dr.

So Sam was only an assistant, just "helping." Like that snot-nosed O'Conner kid who claimed to be in his second year of medical school — home with a broken leg he'd gotten skiing. E.J. was convinced the kid was conning his parents, that he wasn't even in medical school, but he did bring to the table a supply of "people" medical books that he'd brought home from school. Those books now filled a shelf in E.J.'s office — like he really had time right now to read them. But they were at least a resource, to look up basic things like, oh, I don't know, the location of the human appendix, for example. Dogs and cats had no appendix, though the cecum served as an admirable substitute. In about the same position in the abdomen. About.

Bottom line: E.J. Hamilton was in way over his head. He could sew up a cut finger on a person just like he could on a cat's paw, but the human patients he was being asked to *diagnose and treat* ... It was crazy.

"E.J., you okay in there?" Sam called through the door.

"No."

He hit the handle on the toilet and flushed it, then opened the door to face her. "But you found me so I'll have to find a better place to hide next time."

She put her hand on his arm. Didn't say anything, just stood there. That steadied him.

"Grace Tibbits is in Exam One. Kinda for the same reason you were in the bathroom. Hiding. Her family is not taking what's happening to her well."

"And you want *me* to talk to them? Seriously? I have never had to help a dog accept that its mother is dying and I don't think I'd be any good at it."

RAYLYNN BENNETT CALLED out from the reception desk down the hall. "Judd Perkins is on the phone, says he needs to talk to you."

That gave E.J. the escape he was looking for and he headed for his office. "I'll take it in here, Raylynn."

When he picked up the phone, Judd didn't even say hello, just told him: "Something's wrong with Buster."

"What seems to be the trouble?"

Judd began to explain, but at that moment there was a flurry of activity outside in the waiting room and Sam opened his door without knocking. "Becky Sue Potter's here. In early labor. I need your help."

Help *delivering a baby!*

He let that settle for a beat.

Not a litter of kittens. Not a foal or a lamb or a calf. A baby!

"You listening to me?" Judd asked.

"Yeah, sure, Judd. Don't worry about it. Buster'll be fine. If he's still not eating tomorrow morning, bring him in and I'll take a look at him."

"But what about the chicken?"

"What chicken?"

"The chicken Buster killed this morning."

E.J. could hear Becky Sue in the waiting room, moaning.

"I don't do dead-chicken resurrections." E.J. slammed the phone down as Becky Sue let out another cry that at least *sounded* a little like a cow giving birth. There was that.

It wasn't until later — after Sam had determined that Becky Sue's baby was *not* coming today and sent her home, after he'd watched Sam take Reece Tibbits outside for a talk, after he'd sewn up Bud Crocket's finger and put ointment on what was probably poison ivy, *probably*, on Asa Morgan's arm — that E.J. took a breath and thought about Buster and the chicken.

Buster had killed a chicken this morning?

Buster was a big, gentle Great Pyrenees that E.J.'d treated for an infected toenail a couple of years ago. Knew it had to hurt, but the dog hadn't made a sound.

Buster killed a chicken.

Wouldn't touch his kibble but killed a chicken.

"… doing stupid stuff like chewing on rocks …"

E.J. had just gotten seated in his office chair with a cup of fresh coffee that was actually hot, unlike the three cups that'd gotten cold because he'd left them sitting somewhere, when he remembered the rocks part. He got up and went to his filing cabinet, pulled out the drawer and thumbed through the files until he came to the letter P.

Paltrow, Partridge, Pendergrass, Perkins …

He pulled out the chart and ran his finger down the medical history. Then he flipped back to the front page and scanned it again, ran his finger slowly down the list of vaccinations.

Buster had had every one of his shots.

Except one.

E.J. found the phone number at the top of the chart, picked up the phone and called Judd back. Judd didn't answer. He tried again, let it ring and ring. No answer.

"Raylynn, I'm going out for a while," he called out to her. "I'll be back about an hour."

E.J. Hamilton was a veterinarian. No, not a doctor, but he was a vet. A *good* one. The shot Buster was supposed to have taken eighteen months ago but *didn't* was his rabies booster.

Chapter Eight

Viola Tackett watched Malachi disappear into the veterinary clinic, though she was reasonably sure he did not need to come in today to get Sam Sheridan to change the bandage on his wound.

But she'd brought him and dropped him off because he'd asked her to. He seemed better, not so distant, since J-Day, when he'd refused to go home with her when Neb come to get her, stayed to help out, was determined to be a hero.

And what'd it get him? A bullet, that's what. When Viola heard that scrawny little Clayton girl had shot her Malachi — well, it was a good thing for her that her head exploded. 'Cause what Viola woulda done to her if she'd got her hands on the girl woulda been a whole lot worse than that.

As she was bumping along beside Neb on her way home that afternoon, still feeling woozy from whatever it was that thing done to her — the Jabberwock thing — she was already planning. Viola had an intuition about some things. It was that had got her out of trouble with the law all these years, kinda knowing ... not what was gonna happen exactly, just a sense that *something* was going to. That sense had sent her hauling butt away from marijuana patches right before the DEA showed up in their little bug-green helicopters. It'd kept her from getting involved in that deal with them meth-heads. They'd wanted to go in together and she'd said no, while Neb, Obie and Zach was crapping their pants wanting her to say yes. Them meth-heads was undercover cops, and they'd all been in the iron house if she hadn't followed her gut.

Her gut was telling her that the mirage thingy out on the road at the county line wasn't some ... what'd they call it? An atmospheric phenomenon or such as that. Her gut was saying it wasn't gonna blow out of the county quick as it blew in. It was telling her that this was the opportunity of a lifetime.

She understood that once-in-a-lifetime opportunities really did come along only once in a lifetime. And if you didn't drop your beer on the floor, jump up and invite Opportunity in soon's it knocked on your door, it was like to go to the neighbors and see did they welcome it.

Just suppose that Jabberwock thing hung around, didn't go poof in a puff of smoke. Suppose it kept folks from coming and going in and out of Nowhere County for a long time. Suppose it *never* went away. What did that mean?

It meant that Viola Tackett had just been handed her own little kingdom.

Her head had been spinning with plans every waking moment since. She had to be smart, though. Play her cards right. Not make her move until she had all her ducks beak-to-tail-feathers.

She'd borrowed the Martins' old Chevrolet this morning to come into town, so wouldn't none of the boys have to ride in the "sunshine seats" in the back of Viola's remaining pickup truck or in the truck they used for hauling. The Martins lived at the bottom of the hollow and had a telephone. They was good folks. Their girl May Ella and Neb had a thing when they's young. She was even uglier than he was, had that dish face, all mashed in so her chin stuck out far as her nose. Good thing she kept her knees together because Viola didn't think that boy's git was likely to be any smarter than he was. The oldest of her four sons was the dumbest, but not by much. Neb never even learned how to spell his own name. Went to school through fifth grade and never learned that much. Nebuchadnezzar was a mouthful, she'd grant, and she wished she'd named him something different because it did hurt his feelings that he couldn't spell it. Neb got fat before he was twenty-five and that Cunningham boy who lived on Owl Creek Road come courting on May Ella. The two of them had a yard full of kids, last Viola'd heard. Neb'd had a hard row-to-row trying to compete — ugly, fat and stupid was a tough combination to overcome when you's trying to win a woman. The fat part was Neb's own fault. He brought it on himself eating all kinda junk food — Moon Pies and Ho Hos and Ding Dongs that he got at Tucker's Grocery in Killarney.

Junk food like he'd brought home from that little job she'd sent him and Obie to do last week. That boy'd cleaned out every speck of candy he could find on the premises and a case of RC Cola along with what she'd sent them to steal. She'd have kicked his butt over it, but it might actually have helped with their cover. Wouldn't be long now before she wouldn't need to be sneaking around, though. Not long before she could do whatever she wanted right out in the open. Only had to set another couple of ducks in place. Viola Tackett was on the move.

〜

"Does that hurt?" Sam asked.

"Yeah, it hurts!" Malachi made a face like he was in agony.

"Seriously?"

"I'd rather be scalped."

"I didn't mean 'Does it hurt when I pull the tape off?' Of course it hurts then, with all that hair …" But Sam did not want to get into a discussion about the amount of hair on Malachi Tackett's chest. Nope. Definitely did not want to go *there*. "I meant—"

"The bullet hole is healing nicely," he said. "Maybe needs a Band-Aid." He stopped her before she could interrupt. "Okay, two Band-Aids. One for the entrance wound, one for the exit wound. But you do know that's going to mess with my Get Out of Jail Free card."

She nodded, acknowledging the mutual charade. Unless he got a ride to the clinic — his mother and brothers had dropped him off this morning on their way to the grocery store — he'd be stuck on a mountainside with nobody to talk to except his totally dysfunctional family. She'd figured out two weeks ago that staying to help out after his Jabberwock ride — and then trying to save Merrie McClintock from Abby Clayton — had begun a healing in Malachi that she neither understood nor questioned.

As she eased the tape up off his skin — though it would probably have hurt less if she'd just yanked it off — she stole glances at his face, noting how haunted his eyes still looked. The young man who had returned to Nowhere County right before Christmas from war — Sam didn't even know where or who was fighting — was not the same man who'd left. Not that she knew *that* man particularly well. It wasn't like Sam had spent time with Malachi on the few occasions when he had come home over the years on leave. And she certainly never bumped into him on the street. The Tacketts had lived for generations in the mountains around the little town of Killarney in Turkey Neck Hollow. Deep down in the southeastern part of the county, it wasn't a place you went to unless you intended to go there — and they knew you and knew you were coming. You didn't just happen to pass through on your way somewhere else. There was no somewhere else.

The only time Sam had ever been there had been four years before, and she had gone at the express invitation of Viola Tackett. It was the last time she'd seen Malachi when he was ... still Malachi.

The Tackett house was a log cabin deep back in the woods at the end of a gravel road that wound up the side of a mountain. It looked old and tired and well used. Viola's boys — they'd always be her "boys" — still lived at home, which was a bit odd since they were certainly old enough to find a girl and get married and move out. But none of the others had and Malachi was home so seldom he didn't need his own place.

Viola's daughter, Esther Ruth, Essie, had Down syndrome and the two older boys, Neb and Obie, were ... slow. Sam didn't know what the politically correct term for that was anymore, probably not "mildly retarded" — they just weren't the sharpest knives in the drawer. They all looked like their mother, with big, blunt features, wide mouths and deep sunken eyes beneath thick, black eyebrows. The third brother, Zach, was a couple of rungs higher on the intellectual scale than his brothers, had made it almost all the way through high school.

Of course, Sam knew Viola and her boys were engaged in illegal business ventures. There were rumors of a chop shop off Rabbit Run Road, and they had stills all over the mountains. Of course, half the people in Nowhere County had a still. The Tacketts raised weed, were the drug connection for any and all narcotic and addictive substances, fenced stolen property, and were party to uglier, meaner, darker activities that folks only whispered about.

Sam had received a call from Eunice Martin, who lived at the bottom of the mountain below the Tacketts and whose telephone was the Tacketts' connection to the world. Eunice had said Viola needed Sam to "come tend to Neb" because he'd been bitten by a spider — black widow or brown recluse.

By the time Sam saw him, the man was really sick, should have gone to a hospital when he got the bite, and now it was infected, too. One look at that finger and Sam had burst into a diatribe about how Neb could die and should have gotten help sooner. Surprisingly, the three boys and Viola had taken the tongue-lashing with admirable chagrin.

It was when Sam was on her way out to her car after she bandaged the wound that she saw Malachi. He came striding out of the barn and the sight was ... stunning. He was a very good-looking man — broad shoulders, Marine Corps abs, and glossy black hair that fell over his forehead in a widow's peak. His face was almost aristocratic with a wide forehead, high cheekbones and striking blue eyes beneath slender black eyebrows winging up at the corners. But his good looks only formed a small part of his charisma. There was a dangerous bad-boy vibe about him and an easy confidence, painted on a backdrop of being the high school heartthrob to everything in a skirt for three counties around. When he threw a pass — whether the receiver caught it or not didn't matter — all the girls in the stands were on their feet squealing like they were at a rock concert.

Of course, Sam and Malachi had a history that went back before that. They had spent time together as children, unlikely as it would seem, considering their geography. The two of them and Charlie Ryan — McClintock — had done things together, though she had trouble recalling the specifics.

He'd greeted her, smiled, they'd chatted, caught up, and then she'd left. And dreamed about him for the next three days until she went back out to the Tacketts to see to Neb's finger. Malachi was there, actually seemed to have been waiting for her to show up. They'd sat on the porch for a bit, just talking.

The next time she went to the Tacketts, Malachi's leave was up and he was gone. She hadn't seen him again until two weeks ago when she'd stepped out of E.J.'s veterinary hospital and saw him hunkered down behind the bus shelter with a .22, dodging imaginary bullets and scanning a scene only he could see for enemies who weren't there. Gone was the charming man who chatted with her that day four years ago, sitting on the porch with the summer sun high in the blue sky. This man was a lost, haunted soul. The only Malachi Sam had ever known had left the building.

Chapter Nine

Holmes Fischer knew Martha Whittiker wasn't home. He'd hung around in the shade of the walnut tree on the far side of her garage after he got up from his usual spot behind the swing on her front porch. He always left his sleeping accommodations at dawn. Even folks who granted him tacit agreement to curl up under the bush by their front gate would prefer not to see the homeless man when they woke up.

Thursday nights it was Martha Whittiker's porch. Tonight he'd be back in the Methodist church basement. Or should be. But nothing was as it was supposed to be. All life had shifted and changed and the simple, downhill slide of Holmes Fischer into the depths of alcoholism and death had been interrupted two weeks ago when he had reached out to touch his own reflection in a mirage and had been transported to the Middle of Nowhere where he had come very close to choking to death on his own tongue.

Nothing was right in anybody's world now. Everybody was scared and upset. Doing stupid things. Or very smart things designed to look stupid — as in the break-in at

Peetree's Hardware Store. Somebody had burglarized the place and made off with every box of ammunition in the building — for every imaginable kind of gun. Granted, there wasn't much. If you wanted ammunition, or anything else related to your firearm, you had only to go to the Walmart's sporting goods section in Carlisle to avail yourself of everything your heart could possibly desire.

Or you could go on "up Lexington," as the nowhere people put it, the colloquialism that was like fingernails on a blackboard to an English teacher. Gun stores and firearms supplies took up two whole pages in the Yellow Pages in the Lexington telephone book.

Since neither option was open to the residents of Nowhere County since J-Day, it was quick thinking on someone's part to figure out that ammunition was one of those disposable resources that once exhausted was irreplaceable.

It'd looked like teenagers had done it. There was graffiti spraypainted on the walls of the building and the thieves had also stolen all the candy off the rack by the cash register and a case of RC Cola in the back not yet loaded into the soft drink machine.

Fish didn't think it was teenagers, though. He thought somebody wanted the world to *think* it had been teenagers, somebody smart enough to know it wasn't a plan to let folks know how well armed you were in uncertain times such as these.

It wasn't like Willie Peetree had gone in to work the morning after, saw the broken-out window in the door on the back of the building, and immediately called the law. As Sam had pointed out, a good word picture of life in Nowhere County, Kentucky, the first of June 1995 was "When you dial 911, nobody answers."

Willie hadn't even called the sheriff's department until

he'd cleaned up the mess, as far as Fish knew. And he knew quite a lot, actually, because he was a cigar store Indian. He was such a fixture, like a blue mailbox or a fire hydrant that was so familiar you stopped noticing it. People held conversations while Fish sat/leaned/or lay nearby without giving a moment's thought to the fact that he could hear every word.

And what he'd heard in more than one conversation in the past couple of weeks was that Deputy Sheriff Liam Montgomery was doing his dead level best to keep the lid on, but the boy was hopelessly outgunned. Literally. Though it had not yet come to bullets fired, Fish knew it was only a matter of time before it did. And Liam's presence was about as much deterrent to crime as a Doberman puppy guarding the silver.

He was trying, oh my yes, he was, but when you worked the logic out to the end … what could he do? What if he figured out who'd done the deed, stolen the weapons, then what? Go arrest the suspect. Okay, then what? Fish supposed Liam could put the arrested person or persons in the jail, the size-of-a-London-phone-booth building in the Ridge.

But then what? Arraign him? How? No prosecutor, no judge, no courtroom. What good did it do for Liam to find the offenders when there was no system in place, no process by which to detain and determine the guilt or innocence of any individual and no method by which to administer justice to them if you did?

Fish was counting on that.

Oh, he didn't intend to get caught, but even if he did, he'd merely be sucked into all the then-whats that had no answers. Folks were more concerned with looking after themselves and their loved ones than they were in trying to design and implement a whole justice system on the fly.

Yes sir, Fish was counting on that.

He had had the presence of mind to figure out early on that it would not be long before the only resource that mattered to him was in jeopardy — alcohol. And even now, he could only manage to come by enough of it to comb the tangles out of his nerves. He had as quickly as was prudent gone to the residences of people he knew had not been inside the county on J-Day and relieved them of their supplies of alcohol. His meager stockpile, kept in what looked like a broken filing cabinet in the basement of the Methodist church, was being consumed about as fast as he could come by it.

And he had already stripped all the unoccupied homes he could think of. It wasn't like he had a car and could cruise up and down the county roads, looking for unoccupied residences. He could get the booze from the places he could walk to. Whatever other bounty of alcohol might be out there was beyond his reach.

It was bound to come to this, of course, but he genuinely regretted that to feed the monkey on his back he was now forced to steal from people who *were* home. Oh, not home as in *inside* their houses, but home as not somewhere on the other side of the Jabberwock.

Mrs. Martha Whittiker was his first ... he didn't like the word "victim." He had watched her drive away. And he'd peeked in the window of the garage apartment in her backyard to check on Dylan Shaw, her lowlife druggie grandson who lived there rather than in a cardboard box under a bridge. The teenager had been lying on the couch amid all manner of drug paraphernalia and stoned out of his gourd. What was the kid going to do when his drug supply ran out? Clearly, he didn't have sufficient properly firing synapses right now to care.

Fish didn't think Mrs. Whittiker would be gone long,

but it wouldn't take him five minutes to slip in the back door, gather up all the booze and slip back out. In a movie, it'd be called "a daring daylight robbery." For Fish, it was simple self-preservation.

Finding a Piggly Wiggly grocery bag in a kitchen cupboard, he searched the house like a kid looking for Easter eggs. He found half-full bottles of brandy and scotch and a full bottle of wine in a cabinet in the den and an almost-empty bottle of Bailey's alongside an almost-full bottle of Kahlua in the refrigerator.

He opened the cabinet beside the refrigerator and found a bottle of cooking sherry. When he took it out and set it on the counter to load into his Easter basket he spied what was in the back of the cabinet behind it.

Oh my.

He picked up the bottle of Kentucky bourbon and held it reverently. He hadn't had anything as fine as Maker's Mark whiskey in … he didn't even know how long! Seeing the bottle there, its red wax seal broken, but still almost a full bottle — he couldn't help himself, didn't even bother to pour himself a glass, just drank from the bottle. He only took a little sip. Just a little sip.

It went down smooth, so *smooth*. So he took another sip.

His concentrated delight was interrupted by the sound of someone unlocking the front door. It wasn't until then that he realized he had slid down the kitchen wall, clutching the bottle of Maker's Mark, and had been sitting there sampling it in delight for far too long. Mrs. Whittiker was home. He had to get out the back door. But not without the booze.

He turned too fast and dizzily stumbled, but managed to grab the grocery sack he had filled with bottles as he staggered past the kitchen counter on his way to make a hasty retreat—

"Fish?" Mrs. Whittiker sounded both surprised and confused. "Fish, what are you — *Fish!*"

Though a small woman, Mrs. Whittiker was neither frail nor fragile. She marched into the kitchen and confronted him.

"Fish, I am so disappointed … how could you … *steal?*"

"Never meant to take more than a small supply to keep me lubricated." Hoping she'd be impressed by his remorse, he hung his head in shame. At that small movement, a wave of dizziness swept over him. Too much straight whiskey on an empty stomach had unbalanced him.

"Well, you aren't getting lubricated on my good cooking sherry. How will I make chicken and broccoli stir fry?"

She could see him clutching the Maker's Mark bottle to his chest, clearly the most valuable bottle of alcohol on the premises, but she was worried about the pitiful little bottle of sherry.

"You give me that!" She reached for the sherry.

He picked it up off the counter and swung around to hand it to her.

And he never knew exactly what happened then.

The handing-it-to-her motion must have made him dizzy and he stumbled forward with the momentum of the move … just as she was leaning forward, reaching …

But how could he have …?

The room spun like a freakshow funhouse around him as he clutched the bottle of Maker's Mark to his chest. He had to grab hold of the kitchen counter to stay upright. Held on with the hand he'd been using to hold the bottle of sherry.

So where was the sherry?

In fact, where was Martha Whittiker?

He looked around, careful to move his head slowly.

Then he looked down. Martha Whittiker was sprawled on the kitchen floor at his feet with blood pooling around her head.

Had he ... he must have clocked her in the side of the head with the bottle of sherry.

Or maybe he'd tripped and stumbled into her and she'd fallen and hit her head.

Or maybe she ... other explanations eluded him but surely there were many. The why didn't seem nearly as important right now as the what — and that was the fact that Martha Whittiker was lying unconscious on her kitchen floor and he was in possession of her stolen alcohol.

Panic didn't happen. He was too well lubricated for that. But a kind of drunken terror seized him and he grabbed the bag of accumulated booze and made for the back door. He crossed her backyard, slipped between the fence and the garage and hurried away down the side of the fence out of sight.

He made it all the way to the corner and turned before she set up a hue and cry for him.

Only she might still be unconscious. And he'd just left her there.

He shouldn't have done that. Should have tended to her, tried to help her. But he didn't. He just ran, and prayed dear Jesus that she would be alright.

Chapter Ten

Charlie only realized she was staring off into space when she heard Merrie's voice, seeming to come from a long way away.

"*You* not picking up stuff," the child said, her words full of reproach.

And then Charlie was back in the attic of her mother's house, dust motes floating in the beams of sunlight that stabbed through the phlegm of dirt on the attic window.

"You worry about what *you're* picking up. You may be the princess in this castle but I'm the queen."

Merrie began again to gather up the contents of the fallen box.

The picture had sparked a fleeting memory that had suddenly blossomed into a short film strip of former reality, playing in the theatre of Charlie's mind.

MAYBE SHE SHOULDN'T HAVE FOUND SUCH a good place to hide but she wants to win the game. It was all Malachi's idea and then when they drew straws he got the short one so now he's looking for her and Sam. If he finds her, Charlie will have to be "it" and she doesn't want to be. Hiding is more fun.

And playing here in the woods is much more fun than standing around with the other children.

She looks out through the branches of the bush down the hillside toward where she can hear the sound of music and children's voices. With that many kids running around and squealing, the three of them will never be missed. The secret to not getting in trouble is playing by the rules ... well, some of them.

Sam didn't want to do what Malachi suggested but she had to as soon as Charlie sided with Malachi, because they have to stay together. That's the rule! If the teacher sees one of them by themselves, she'll ask where the other two are because that's the reason they were divided into three-kid groups.

Alphabetically: Ryan, Sheridan, Tackett.

The teacher said on the bus that the three-kid part was so if one got hurt there would be one other kid to stay with the first one that got hurt and a third kid to go for help.

Got hurt? How could you get hurt standing around looking at a bunch of boring stuff? Fake history is what Sam called it. Grownups in costumes showing how to make butter and how to make thread out of wool and then somehow the wool becomes a shirt but Charlie doesn't think they show that part.

Sam was as bored as Charlie and Malachi so even if she didn't want to play at first, Charlie was sure she was glad to get away.

Charlie wonders where Sam is hiding.

Hide-and-seek would have been a blast if they could have played in all the empty buildings. There would have been like a ba-gillian places to hide, but the kids aren't allowed to go into the buildings because they're old and falling down and not safe. Teachers take one group after another of the children to look around the houses and describe who might have lived there, but the exhibits are set up in the empty space in front of the buildings. Kids were not allowed to leave that area — they'd spot you if you tried to sneak away. So they'd had to settle for hiding somewhere among the exhibit booths. As soon as Malachi closed his eyes and started counting, Charlie had taken off into the woods behind where the woman was churning butter, found a great big oleander bush and hunkered down behind it. She's not far from the booth, not far at all.

Maybe a teacher caught Sam or Malachi and now they're all in trouble for not staying together and—

No, if they'd gotten caught, the teachers would be looking for her, calling for her.

They'd agreed that big tree with the funny-looking bent limb was olly olly oxen free — the tree behind the booth where a man with a fake beard that's coming unglued on one side is whittling something.

Charlie wonders if she should leave her hiding place and run for the tree when she sees Sam coming up the hillside, sneaking from one tree to the next. Sam sees Charlie at the same time she hears something behind her — it's Malachi! Sam runs to a big oak tree that's on the other side of a bare spot in the woods from the bush where she's hiding.

"I see you," Malachi calls out, but Charlie doesn't know which one of them he means.

Sam motions to Charlie, telling her to stand up.

Both she and Sam step out of their hiding places into the clear spot.

Malachi sees them. He has to catch one of them and tag them, but he can't chase them both at the same time.

"You can't catch me!" Sam cries and runs off into the woods to her right, giggling.

Malachi starts after her when Charlie cries out the same thing, and runs in the opposite direction. She's giggling, too, wondering which one of them he'll chose to chase. She looks over her shoulder and sees that it's Sam, so she stops.

"Hey Malachi, over here!" He stops and turns her way and she waves her hand. "Can't catch ME," she cries and the look on his face … she laughs out loud then.

She turns and runs away and Malachi must have changed his mind about Sam and come after Charlie because she hears a sound far off to the right. Sam's laughing.

"Yo, Malachi," Sam cries. "Mallllll-a-chiiiiii."

It's faint, but Charlie can hear the bluegrass music from down below as she runs, mingled with the hum of the crowd. There's a pause, and then the fiddler cranks up "Cotton-Eyed Joe," Charlie's favorite, and she turns toward the familiar sound, looks down the mountainside. She can see Sam below her, but Sam's not running or hiding. She's just standing there, looking at something farther up the hillside beyond Charlie.

Charlie turns around to see what Sam might be looking at.

Mist.

It flows down the mountainside as fast as an avalanche, white like snow and almost as thick. Charlie doesn't have time to do anything before the mist is on her, all around her, erasing the world.

THEN THE MEMORY WAS GONE. It flashed through Charlie's mind like a comet, bright and shining and then gone.

What was *that* about?

She turned the picture over in her hand to see if anything was written on the back. Nothing.

It seemed somehow odd that she didn't remember playing with Sam and Malachi when they were children, but maybe they didn't play together at all, maybe it was just the luck of the draw, the alphabet, that had put them together that one time and never again.

The luck of the *alphabet*. She smiled. Well, duh. Charlie thought of a writer's mind like a gigantic attic, where everything she'd ever seen or thought or imagined or experienced was tucked away somewhere, for use whenever she happened to stumble upon it.

She turned the picture back over and tried to see what

might be in the background of it. It was just the dilapidated wooden porch steps in front of a shack. One of the falling-down structures in the ghost town. Maybe every group of three kids got their pictures taken together in front of it.

She glanced up to see that Merrie had abandoned the task of picking up the spilled paper and had something in her hand.

"Where'd you get that?"

"Finded it here. It's shiny."

Merrie held out a rock to Charlie and what looked like a lump of ugly rock was actually a geode. Charlie had taken geology the lone year she was in college. Flunked it, but still she'd learned that much. It was a small piece that'd been broken off a pretty good-sized geode.

What was a geode doing in a box of school keepsakes? Was it Mallory's? Where did she get it? This was coal country and geodes were rare here. She'd been to Colorado once, wandered around touristy rock stores where all sorts of gemstones, geodes, crystals, and polished granite were on sale, but this one wasn't grand enough to be sold in a store. She didn't think it was Mallory's. It belonged to Charlie. She didn't know how she knew that, but she did. She was almost certain this was the rock that the old woman she had remembered had given to her. What old woman? Where?

Then she turned the picture back over, examined it. The three children were not really smiling. They were doing that thing kids do when you tell them, "Smile for the camera." So they pull back the corners of their mouths because they've been told to.

Charlie got up from where she was seated and went to the window, let the bright sunlight fall on the picture so she could study it. Nope, those kids definitely were not smiling.

They were looking into the camera with fake smiles stuck like name tags on their faces. But their eyes. The looks in their eyes. They looked frightened.

Frightened? Oh, come on. That was just her imagination. How could you tell a smiling kid was frightened just from a picture?

Where had Charlie gotten the picture?

Little moths of memories fluttered around the light in the attic of her mind. They had been on a school bus with a teacher. She couldn't recall the woman's name but she wasn't Charlie's teacher. She couldn't even remember if she and Sam and Malachi had been in the same classroom, but she didn't think so. Not Malachi, anyway. She and Sam had been in the same classroom often as children, had become besties — friends in later elementary school, like third, fourth and fifth grades — and had sat together during recess with their dolls, playing "babies." But this picture was taken when they were much younger. Where had they been taken in a school bus where somebody was making butter in a churn, somebody else was making thread on a loom?

Some kind of "pioneer demonstration," some place that had been set up with people demonstrating traditional mountain crafts. There had been music! She remembered now. A fiddle and a banjo, classic instruments like a dulcimer and a mandolin, and an old man with a beard had been playing the spoons, tapping his foot and spitting his tobacco juice on the ground. Folk music. Bluegrass music. And dancing. That was vague, but weren't there cloggers? Or was she remembering the county fair, which had stopped being a fair when she was in fourth or fifth grade, but they always had cloggers there and bluegrass music.

Another image comets through her mind and then is gone.

Fingers wrapped tight around her upper arm. Bad breath in her face. The old woman is shaking her.

Even now, standing in the dust-mote-speckled beam of sunlight streaming in the window, Charlie felt a cold chill wash over her. She'd been scared to death of the woman. *The woman had given her a rock.*

She stood for a moment longer, then strode across the paper still spilled on the floor and unlatched the door to the attic.

"Come on, doodle bug," she said to Merrie. "We're going for a ride."

Chapter Eleven

When Harry Tungate tore out down the road away from Abner Riley's house, he had no destination in mind. He wasn't going *to* anywhere. He was going *away from* … from that whatever it was.

Roscoe.

Of course, Roscoe.

They were identical twins who had changed some as they'd grown older. Get the two of them together, though, and it was obvious.

They never been close by most people's definition of close because they didn't have to be. Ordinary brothers spent time with each other, maybe went out and did things together, talked on the phone, things like that.

Harry and Roscoe probably didn't talk more than once or twice a month. And since neither of them was a chitchat kind of man, when they did talk there was a reason. Harry needed Roscoe's help to move a chifforobe. Roscoe wanted Harry to fix a broke-down car. Harry was better at mechanical things than Roscoe.

It had taken only a phone call and a couple of terse

sentences to plan the fishing trip that had sent them across the county line on J-Day, looking to find their cousin who was supposed to bring the beer.

And both of them had married good women, had been good husbands so they'd been close to their wives. They'd also buried their wives within two years of each other. Roscoe's wife, Miriam, had died of ALS and he'd got a hospital bed and moved it into his living room so he and his daughters could care for her at home until she died.

What others might take for a lack of closeness was exactly the opposite. Harry and Roscoe didn't have to see each other, talk to each other, do things together to be close. They just were. If people knew how close they actually were, they might be creeped out by it.

When they were kids they could finish each other's sentences as soon as they could talk, and had developed their own twin language that baffled and infuriated their parents. The experts would tell you that in any twin relationship, one is the dominant twin and the other the follower. Well in fifty-six years of breathing air on the planet, neither Roscoe nor Harry had ever given an inch to the other. They were both dominant, and it would have caused explosive disagreements, each determined to be the big gun and be right, except they didn't disagree. What one thought, the other did, too. They got in each other's faces sometimes about how to do whatever it was they'd decided to do, but neither Harry nor Roscoe came out on top of all the disputes. They were evenly matched.

And though neither of them had ever even admitted it to each other, there were times when they knew the other's thoughts. Oh, not just knew that Roscoe would say this because that's just how Roscoe was. Or because that's what Harry would have said so of course it was what Roscoe'd say.

More than that.

Harry hit his thumb with a hammer building a back porch and Roscoe knew it. *Felt it.* Called Bea while it was still throbbing to tell her she'd ought to put ice on it. Harry had "heard" Roscoe tell the Jentry brothers to leave him alone when they were bullying him in the eighth grade and Harry had come running down the hall from the gym in his shorts to defend his brother.

It happened so often, and in so many different ways, it was a silent communication they both took for granted and never questioned. So when Harry pulled his truck to a stop in the driveway of Roscoe's house on Burnt Stump Road, he knew Roscoe'd be on the porch waiting for him.

Didn't take but a couple of sentences to tell the story because Roscoe'd felt Harry's fear.

"It *breathed*?" Roscoe said.

"Yeah, it breathed!"

"How you know you wasn't hallucinating or something?"

"You know I wasn't." Yeah, Roscoe knew.

"Well, then, I guess we'd best go see what's happened to Abner."

"I ain't going back there."

He knew Roscoe wouldn't either.

"Then what …?"

"We got to *tell* somebody." Harry was only just now able to speak without his voice shaking. "Liam, I guess. Or … I don't know."

"Tell him Abner's missing? That's all?"

"Depends."

"On what?"

"On who we tell."

Without consulting, Roscoe went around to the passenger door of Harry's truck and got in.

"Yeah," Harry said, in response to a question Roscoe didn't ask. "They'll be in the Middle of Nowhere."

THE OLDEST OF Grace Tibbits's three children, Reece, had married young and stupid and now spent his days working in his woodshop so he wouldn't have to listen to his wimpy wife's incessant whining. His mama had warned him, but he wouldn't listen.

Maybe his mother had been the reason he'd picked Cissy, maybe there was some stupid rebellious streak in him and he went looking for his mother's polar opposite.

Well, he'd found her. What an idiot.

At fifty-five, Reece was gruff but not callous, a decent tough-guy who would tell a man he was going to beat the crap out of him before he did it, then he'd hold out a hand to help the guy up off the ground when he was done.

The most remarkable thing about Reece was that there was nothing remarkable about him at all. And he liked that, was proud of being "ordinary." Average height, average weight, easily forgettable face. Sometimes he thought he'd missed his calling — should have made a career out of holding up liquor stores because nobody would have been able to pick him out of a lineup. Well — except for the lightning bolt of pure white hair that extended through his black hair from his brow line to his collar.

His mother was a strong woman, she was a Proverbs 31 woman, the one described in Scripture as the perfect wife. When he'd first heard that in church he'd thought what a shame it was his father had been killed at sea instead of enjoying a life alongside his mother. Verse 28 of that chapter had stuck with him all these years ... "and her children shall rise up and call her blessed."

He'd never in his life met another woman, another human being, as ... as everything as his mother. Bright, funny, strong, gentle, loving ...

Crap, the list went on forever. He'd thought about it ever since she had announced on Super Bowl Sunday that she would be going to Carlisle twice a week for dialysis.

Said it like, "Hand me the mashed potatoes."

The whole family had gathered to watch the San Diego Chargers kick the butts of the San Francisco 49ers — which they didn't, by the way — and he and his little brother, his sisters and assorted in-laws and grandchildren were dumbstruck. His mother had never mentioned to them that she had anything wrong with her kidneys. And suddenly there she was saying she had to use a machine because her kidneys were, her words, "shriveled up and useless."

Reece changed after that, his outlook did anyway. He had taken for granted his whole life how amazing his mother was, like every other oldest son on the planet. And because she was so strong, he never put her and "mortality" in the same paragraph.

Her dialysis had been a wake-up call. And because he was a carpenter, set his own hours, he'd insisted on driving her to every one of her dialysis appointments.

Which had put the two of them in the car together when they crossed over into Beaufort County, or tried to, on Jabberwock Day.

He had been *so sick* when he came around and found himself at the bus shelter. Sam Sheridan had said that the phenomenon or whatever it was affected everybody differently, and he was one of the unfortunate few who was debilitated by vomiting and migraine-like headaches for the whole rest of that day and into the night. Hadn't even realized his mother'd stayed at the Dollar Store parking lot to help out until Cissy whined about having to go pick her up the next morning.

The implications of the Jabberwock were slow to sink in with Reece. Whatever it was, it'd go away, be gone by tomorrow. Tuesday at the latest. It had appeared out of nowhere and it would vanish back into the nowhere just as quickly.

But it didn't. And now it was killing his mother.

There was nothing wrong with her! Okay, she'd done irreparable damage to her kidneys with Ibuprofen years ago. Called it "vitamin I," just like all the other runners did. Took it religiously every day and sometimes more often than that so she could run her daily five-mile route and compete in 5K and 10K races. Nobody knew then, or at least nobody had said at the time, that constant use of that kind of anti-inflammatory drug could have dangerous side effects.

She'd explained all that to him and his sisters during the stupid Indiana Jones halftime show after she'd made the dialysis announcement. Said she'd had no idea she had a problem until a routine physical had turned up a dangerously high creatinine level in her blood. By then, she was already in stage two kidney disease and after another couple of decades, her kidneys almost completely ceased functioning

He had brought up the possibility of a kidney transplant and his mother almost bit his head off just for suggesting it. If he thought she was going to take a kidney from one of her healthy children just so she didn't have to drive to Carlisle twice a week, he had a whole bunch of other thinks coming!

Other than the time out of her life she spent hooked

up to the machine — and she used it to read, was teaching herself Mandarin Chinese, for crying out loud — she was as healthy as she had ever been. She said dialysis "scrubbed her blood and hung it out on the line to dry in the sun."

With dialysis, his mother led a normal life. Without it, she would die.

The Jabberwock had built a wall around the county — nobody in or out — and that wall was killing his mother.

The Jabberwock was killing his mother.

And Reece Tibbits flat out would *not* allow that to happen, not as long as he had breath in his body.

He'd been surprised and disappointed by the reactions of everybody else — who seemed to be content to hang out here in Nowhere County for a couple of weeks or months or however long it was until the Jabberwock thing blew back out again as strangely as it had blown in. All those people — they didn't have any skin in the game. The ones sucking on the government welfare check teat never went anywhere anyway, might be a few of them up in the hollows somewhere who didn't even know yet they couldn't leave because they hadn't tried.

Even folks he respected — Sam Sheridan and Deputy Montgomery, the veterinarian, E.J. Hamilton. All they did was talk about it. They wanted to *understand* it, figure out how it got here and why.

Nobody said anything about doing something about it. Nobody was talking about *getting rid of the thing*.

When he brought up the subject, people looked at him like he was crazy. He hadn't lost his mind. All he had lost was sleep — probably hadn't slept more than a couple of hours a night since they'd hauled him home and put him to bed on J-Day.

How could he sleep once he figured out the Jabberwock was lethal? How could anybody?

And all that missed sleep had dulled his thinking, he'd grant that. It'd made him irritable and a little paranoid, too — he recognized those things in rare moments of clarity, but wouldn't acknowledge any permanent changes in his ability to think and reason.

Certainly nothing that dulled his ability to plan because he *had* planned, had figured out how to fight back. Today — tomorrow at the latest — he and that Jabberwock were going to lock horns. He was going to kick its butt the way the Chargers hadn't kicked the 49ers' butts and send it back where it came from! His mother was getting sicker by the day.

He would not let his mother die!

Chapter Twelve

The wound had been an excuse to go to the clinic and Malachi told himself that as long as he knew it was an excuse, as long as he didn't engage in self-deception, believe his own lie, he'd be fine. The loonies in the rubber rooms who had aluminum foil in their hats were running from reality. Malachi did not number among those so afflicted.

He knew that he'd come to the clinic because it was only when he was actively involved in dealing with the catastrophe that had struck the county two weeks ago, helping — even if all he did was hose vomit off into the creek — he could ease out from under the weight he carried, set it aside. Part of it was just being needed. He was part of the solution here. He could do something about the carnage, actually help those who were suffering. He didn't have to stand there with chains on his uniform — his *orders* and his *duty* — keeping him from even trying to help.

And Malachi was able to relax in the company of the "home folks." He didn't share battle memories with them,

hadn't been standing beside them, looking at the unthink-
able so that it was forever afterward painful to make full
eye contact. Looks *there* were too knowing.

Sam stepped away from him and took off her gloves
just as there was a knock at the door and Charlie opened it
just enough to stick her head inside.

"Raylynn said you were in here—" She stopped when
she saw Malachi. "I'm sorry, Raylynn didn't say anything
about—"

"Band-Aids," he interrupted and gestured toward his
side as he lifted his shirt off the table and began putting it
on. "Not major surgery. Band-Aids."

"I'll come back later," Charlie began and then seemed
to change her mind. "Actually, finding you here …" She
looked at Sam. "Could we talk? Just for a few minutes. I
brought something to show you and I think Malachi might
be interested, too."

Sam smiled.

"Actually, the waiting room's empty and E.J. went
running out of here like his hair was on fire a few minutes
ago, didn't say where he was going or when he'd be back."
She looked at her watch. "Almost noon. I declare it
lunchtime. E.J. usually has sandwich makings upstairs in
his kitchen. *If* he still has bread we could—"

"Maybe later. This won't take long."

"The breakroom it is, then."

They stepped out into the hallway. Merrie was at the
other end, following Raylynn into the "hospital" where the
menagerie was housed. She gave Charlie a stricken look.

"S'okay," Charlie called out to her. "You can help miss
Raylynn feed the puppies." To Raylynn she said, "Bring
her back when she wears you out."

"Are you kidding? She's way cuter than the puppies."

The breakroom really wasn't. It was a storage room,

windowless and cheerless, where Raylynn had set up a card table and a couple of folding chairs. A stack of canned dog food boxes had been commandeered for use as a coffee pot stand and Styrofoam cups sat beside it along with a paper cup filled with packets of artificial sweetener.

"It's not much, but we call it home," Sam said and flashed her solitary dimple.

Malachi took passing note of how each of the women in the room was … singular, impressive in her own unique way. Sam looked like her face belonged on a cereal box and Charlie was drop-dead gorgeous. Both of them had a presence and he didn't think either one of them was aware of it, which, of course, magnified the effect by a factor of ten.

He took the chair against the far wall, spun it around and straddled it, resting his forearms on the back. Sam sat down next to him. Charlie stood across from them both. She reached into her purse and took something out and placed it on the table between them.

"See anybody you know?"

Malachi picked up the photograph of three grinning children and held it up so he and Sam could both look at it.

A memory rode into his mind on the back of recognition.

WHEN MALACHI FINISHES COUNTING to a hundred by fives, he looks up and he sees Charlie run off behind that booth where a lady's churning butter, and then up into the woods. That's cheating! They're not supposed to leave the grounds where all the booths are set up that has a big word in the name that he can't remember, something that sounds like "rinny sauce."

But they aren't supposed to be running around playing hide-and-

seek either! So he supposes if they're breaking the rule about playing the game instead of looking at the exhibits, it doesn't matter if they break the other rule about not leaving the grounds.

He looks around, doesn't see Sam anywhere. He is "it" and must find and tag one of the other two, and keep them for making a break for the big tree with the funny-looking bent limb at the edge of town, by the sign that says "Gideon." That's home base. If he doesn't tag them before they can run to that tree and cry "olly olly oxen free," he will have to stay "it," and it's way more fun to hide.

If he stays near the tree, no matter where they're hiding, when Charlie and Sam come out to run for home base, he'll see them. He's faster than either of them — they're just girls — and he can tag one of them before they get to the tree and then they'll be it and he can go hide.

But he saw where Charlie went into the woods and he's sure he can find her there. Nothing to hide behind but trees.

If he leaves home base, though, he runs the risk of Sam racing to it and touching it before he can catch her.

But if he finds Charlie, that won't matter because he'll tag her and she'll be it and he can go hide the next round.

He casts another look around. Sam is easy to spot with all that red hair, but he doesn't see her anywhere. With a final look at the home base tree, he darts around the other children, behind the booth of the churning woman and off into the woods where Charlie went.

Chapter Thirteen

Judd stood with his back against the barn door as the huge dog tried to claw his way in. The animal lunged at the door — *bam!* — and the latch held, but it might not have if Judd's body hadn't been taking most of the weight of the blows.

The dog's growl was the single most horrifying sound Judd had ever heard. And as the growling animal threw himself at the door again and again, his growling wasn't the only sound in Judd's ears. Judd could hear crying, sobbing. And at first he didn't even realize he was the one blubbering. Not in fear now that he was safe in here, where the lunging beast couldn't get to him. Now, he was crying in sorrow, mourning the loss of the beautiful, gentle dog that crawled into Judd's bed at night when it was especially cold in the winter, cuddled up next to Judd ... not because the dog was cold — in that fur coat! No, he did it to keep Judd warm.

Buster couldn't do tricks, not like some other dogs. Mildred taught him the German commands out of that book, but once she got sick, Judd didn't have the time or the energy to put into teaching him to roll over or beg or shake hands or such as that. Buster learned stuff just by watching, though. He'd sit when Judd held his palm out and Judd realized he'd figured out that's what Judd wanted cause he held his hand out like that to keep the dog from jumping up for his food. He'd lie down on the floor when you told him. He'd get off the furniture when you told him, didn't "respond to Judd's commands," just done what Judd said to do.

Buster loved to chase butterflies in the meadow in the spring, and seeing that big white dog galumphing through the flowers, pollen going every which way, was one of the best sights in the world. He was afraid of thunderstorms, hid under the bed, liked ice cubes and learned to catch them when you tossed them to him, and he could look as pitiful as a baby seal when you scolded him.

Buster was the best dog there ever was! Judd loved him fiercely.

The beast on the other side of the barn door, launching himself at it again and again, wasn't Buster. Soon's Judd seen the foamy stuff dripping off his lower lip, and him walking down the hillside kinda crooked-like, he knew. He didn't have time to think what he'd ought to do because Buster seen him and *charged*. Judd made it to the barn and got the door slammed and latched not two seconds before Buster crashed into it like 170 pounds of crazed beast.

Judd's heart was hammering, and he was gasping for air like he'd run a mile instead of just sprinted across the barnyard to the barn door — the closest place of safety he could see. As he stood there, panting, his body jolted forward again and again by Buster charging, he figured he should have made a run for the house. But he hadn't had time to think. The barn was closer, and might be Buster could have broken through the back door of the house. His old truck was parked on the other side of the barnyard and he never woulda made it that far. Besides, his keys was in the house.

He was gonna have to calm down some and think what to do, but right now he was so upset his mind was flitting from one thing to another like them hummingbirds that come to dip they little beaks into that red bird feeder that Mildred used to put sugar water in, so she could stand at the sink in the evening and watch the birds while she was doing the supper dishes.

Judd had meant to keep sugar water in that thing, meant to do a lot of things that just kinda slipped away after Millie passed. By the time he thought how he'd ought to go out there and put sugar water in the thing it had been dried up for months. He filled it up, but them hummingbirds never did come back.

Bam!

Buster lunged into the door again and liked to knocked Judd over onto the floor. With Judd's back braced against the door, it wouldn't take that dog more than three or four good lunges and the latch'd break, or the screws would come out of that old barn wood or the door might come off the hinges altogether.

It wasn't a very big barn and it was old, the wood dry, the outside gray from sun and rain. The big barn was where he hung tobacco from that little bit of tobacco acreage he had, but it was painted black and back farther from the house. This barn was just to put his tractor in, store feed for the chickens and hay, had double doors on the front that opened out big enough to drive farm machinery through, a ladder up into the hayloft and bay doors in the hayloft. Couldn't open but one of them, though. There was a piece of clothesline wire that hooked the doors to the frames so they didn't flop open. Without the wire, there wasn't no way to shut them — unless you could stand out there in midair like you's Wile E. Coyote when he run out there past the edge of a cliff. The clothes-line wire on the door on the right had broke and he hadn't got around to fixing it yet so if you opened it wasn't no way to get it closed.

Bam!

Buster hit the door again.

They was a lot of things Judd hadn't got around to, couldn't seem to think clear without Millie there to push him off in the right direction.

He'd been thinking about that, about how he had been kinda walking around in a cloud since they put her in the ground. Hadn't had his head on right and couldn't think, let things drop, fall through the cracks. Like that clothesline wire.

And like Buster's shots.

Millie always took care of things like that. When they'd got him, she was determined to let him stay in the house. Cute little white puppy. He didn't stay little long, and he shed so much white fur all over everything, Millie'd said once if she saved all the fur she swept up in a week she'd have enough to make a whole new dog. Since Great Pyrenees were originally bred for guarding livestock, they was used to thinking on their own — that's what E.J.'d said when they'd took him in for puppy shots and Millie had complained that he still wasn't house broke. E.J.'d told her she had to be patient, had to be firm and consistent and if there was anything in the world that woman was it was consistent. Wasn't long before she'd got that dog to go stand at the back door when he needed to go out. She'd wanted to get a doggie door so he could do it on his own, but wasn't a doggie door big enough for him by the time he was seven or eight months old. She'd finally give up and let go of her "house dog" dream, put a bed for him on the porch and for a while there, before she got sick, you could put on a pair of black dress pants on Sunday without having to use duct tape to pull all the dog hair off.

After Millie was gone, Judd brought Buster back in and let him be a house dog, didn't care how much he shed on the furniture. Didn't even think about it, like he didn't keep track of stuff you had to do at a certain time. Millie'd wrote everything down on the calendar that was stuck to the refrigerator with a magnet from Niagara Falls, where they'd gone on vacation a couple of years ago. He'd glanced at that calendar when he was waiting for E.J. to pick up and seen it was still on February. He hadn't put nothing on it nor tore any of the pages off since then.

Bam!

Rabies.

Even the word was ugly and scary. Mad dog. Wasn't no other explanation for it and Buster was all the time out in the woods, chasing one varmint or another. Foxes was carriers, Judd had heard. Bats and skunks and possums. And now that he thought about it the bottom dropped out of his stomach because he *remembered*. Buster'd come back to the house a week ago Thursday and he had scratches on his snout. Judd'd wondered what he'd tangled with, and thought "you shoulda seen the other guy."

That was it? Buster'd got bit and because Judd hadn't had the sense to get him in to E.J. on time for his booster shot …

He made a sound in his throat that was a kind of snorting sob. *His fault.* Buster was gonna have to be put down and wasn't nobody in the world to blame but himself.

He noticed then that Buster wasn't jumping at the door anymore.

Them times when he thought Buster could read his mind — well, right now Judd thought he could read Buster's. Judd looked across the barn to that hole where he hadn't been watching what he was doing and hit the barn with the tobacco setter. Knocked some boards out. It was big enough—

Buster's snarling snout stuck through the opening, then his whole body crashed into it. Wouldn't take much to break through them weak boards. Not much at all.

Chapter Fourteen

"You cheated," Malachi told Charlie. She'd handed him a picture of the three of them in first grade and those were the first words out of his mouth after he looked at it.

"Cheated? What are you talking about?"

Sam studied the picture, trying to imagine the other two with missing front teeth, scabs riding their knees, little kids. "I didn't even know we played together," she said.

"Do you remember this?" Malachi tapped the picture. Sam shook her head.

"Let's loop back around here … what do you mean I cheated?"

"You did. We weren't allowed to go out beyond the booths, and you went running off into the woods."

A light came on in Sam's head and she *did* remember. "The whole school went."

"Not just our school. All the counties around. We had to get permission slips and my mother did not have any desire to see her baby boy hauled off into the ghost town in Fearsome Hollow."

"That's where we were?" Charlie asked.

"Yeah. It was some kind of—" He smiled. "I thought it sounded like *rinny sauce*, must have been a Renaissance Fair. I don't know who set it up but it was in Gideon. And all the elementary schools from the counties around brought kids in busses."

"I remember being in the bus and Mrs. ... I don't remember her name, she wasn't my teacher, but she said we all had to remain in groups of three." Charlie parroted, "'... if one of you gets hurt—'"

"You know, gets struck by lightning," Malachi put in.

"Is attacked by a crocodile," Sam said.

Charlie plowed ahead, "... then one of the three can stay with the one whose arm was bitten off by a pterodactyl, while the third child goes for help."

"That's why we were together," Malachi said. "Alphabetical order by last name: R, S and T." He paused. "Wasn't E.J. in our class? I don't remember him being there that day, but he'd have been hanging out with the Gibson twins and Chloe Inman."

"If he'd been with us, *that* would have changed the dynamic. E.J. *never* would have suggested breaking the rules," Charlie said.

"Big doors swing on little hinges," Sam said.

"I must have remembered that whole thing, stored it somewhere in my head and it was the origin of *The Alphabet Gang*."

Sam's head snapped up.

"Whooooa. *The Alphabet Gang?*" The puzzle pieces fell into place. Charlie had said she was a writer, but it'd never occurred to Sam she'd meant *fiction*. Sam assumed she wrote ... you know, reports for some big company, or brochures, or textbooks or ... but children's books! And not just any children's books. "*You're* ... C.R.R. Underhill?"

Malachi looked puzzled, but even he ... "Isn't that the writer—"

"Of the most popular children's books in the country! The ones they made into that cartoon series — three little kids who fight dragons." Sam's smile grew wider. "Two little girls and a little boy and Bonnie has red ... is that *me*?"

"Busted. And yeah, I guess she is you, because it's clear from this" — she gestured at the picture — "where the idea came from. Allie. Bonnie. Caleb. AKA Ryan, Sheridan and Tackett."

"So we're famous?" Malachi wanted to know. "Okay, *we're* not famous, but *you* are ... C.R.R. ... Charlene Reneé Ryan *Underhill*."

"You know where I got that, don't you?"

Of course Sam knew. She might not remember the three of them playing together as children, but they'd been 'a thing' their senior year in high school when Mr. Fischer taught the whole year on *The Lord of the Rings*. The three of them had become Tolkien groupies.

"The name Gandalf gave Frodo, told him to check into the inn in Bree using the name 'Underhill ... if any name must be given.'"

"So when the black riders showed up, they were looking for Baggins," Malachi said. "They'd come all the way from Mordor—"

"Where the shadows lie." Charlie tried to sound like James Earl Jones. "And speaking of shadows, do you guys remember the mist that day?"

"No," Sam said. "Wait, yes ... the mist. I remember. It came down the hillside, through the trees."

"Where we weren't *supposed to be*," Malachi said, giving Charlie the eye.

"Yeah, we weren't allowed to leave the area where

they'd set up the booths demonstrating things like how to churn butter—"

"—or how to bang on a horseshoe and flatten it on an anvil," Malachi said. "That particular exhibit was the only one that interested me, but it was a total bomb. Even at — what, seven years old? — I knew there had to be a forge to heat the horseshoe. But there was nothing but a burley guy in an apron, banging on a horseshoe he was holding unnecessarily in tongs. Every once in a while, he'd dip the unheated horseshoe in water. Fail." He turned again to Charlie. "But you left the grounds to hide. That was cheating."

"I just remember the three of us decided to play hide-and-seek because the exhibits were boring," Charlie said.

"No," Sam said to Malachi, "*you* decided you wanted to play hide-and-seek."

"And you went right along with him."

"No, I didn't. I wanted to be a good little girl."

"But you also didn't want to be a lone fish," Charlie said. "The kid who had to explain to whatever grownup seined you out of the sea of threesomes what had happened to the other two."

"True that," Sam admitted.

"And you saw the mist coming," Charlie told her. "I turned around and it was just there."

"It was there … and nothing else was," Malachi said, echoing the memories that had bloomed in Sam's head. "It was so thick you couldn't see—"

"Your hand in front of your face," Charlie said.

"But you could still hear, and I heard you guys' voices," Sam said. "But they were soft, whispers."

"Why would we have been whispering?" Malachi said. "But I did *hear* whispers. And a voice that didn't sound like a girl's."

"I heard you, Malachi," Charlie said. "Had to be you. I couldn't hear what you were saying, but I followed you, calling out. But you never answered."

"I'd forgotten about this, about all of it."

Sam hadn't even remembered they'd played together, certainly not that field trip, or hide-and-seek in the woods, and when she finally did, it was like she had to pry the memories loose to see them. They were bound up tight, didn't want to let go. And wrapped around them was a fear she couldn't explain.

She marveled at the wonder in her own voice. "I got lost in the woods, couldn't see anything, followed your voices but couldn't find you. I was scared."

"Not just lost, but lost for a long time," Malachi said.

"For hours," Charlie said. "Wandering up and down the hills. I fell and skinned my knee, scratched my face … I was bawling and calling out and trying to hear somebody answer."

"I was so scared, called until my throat was raw and my voice was hoarse. And as soon as I'd start crying, I'd hear you guys whispering again and it sounded like you were so close … just right there."

All three fell silent.

"Anybody besides me putting all this together?" Malachi asked, his voice soft, maybe even airless.

Sam was and she didn't like where it was leading.

"I wasn't whispering," she said.

"Neither was I," Charlie said.

"Make that three," Malachi said.

"I called out for you guys — 'Charlie! Malachi! Where are you?' as loud as I could yell. Over and over, but you never answered."

"I never heard anybody call my name," Charlie said.

"Make that three of a kind again," said Malachi. "Beats two pairs, if we were playing poker."

There was another silence.

"Sooooo ..." Malachi said, "none of us whispered, but all of us *heard* whispers. All of us called out, but none of us ever heard our own name. And we were in an area ... what? Surely smaller than a football field."

"Then the old lady was just there. Came out of the mist," Charlie said.

"Old lady?" Sam said.

"You don't remember an old lady?"

"You do?"

"So do I," said Malachi.

"What ... she just *appeared*, burst full grown from an oak tree like Tecumseh?" Sam said.

"I saw you with the old lady," Malachi said. "She grabbed you by the arm. And brave boy that I was, I leapt out of the bushes with a sword."

"A sword?"

"Okay, a whip, like Indiana Jones."

"Fail," Sam and Charlie said at the same time.

"You didn't leap out of the woods at all," Charlie said. "She found you like she found me and Sam. You were just as lost."

"I don't remember any old lady," Sam said. "You're making that up."

Charlie sat down then for the first time, "No, I'm not. I have not thought about that day in the past ... do the math, twenty-five years? Not once until I saw that picture."

"I hadn't thought about it until five minutes ago," said Sam.

"I've thought about it," Malachi said and the two turned to look at him.

"You don't remember what she said to us?" he asked,

looking from one to the other. "About the town vanishing … you don't remember?"

"You're serious? You had a conversation with an old lady in the woods?"

"*We* had a conversation," he said. "All three of us were there, in mist so thick it was like standing in milk."

"I do *not* remember an old woman," Sam said, adamant. "Who was she?"

"At the time, we didn't know," Malachi said. "But now I have a good guess."

"You don't think … we actually talked to the Gideon Witch?" Sam was incredulous.

"Well, she looked pretty witch-y to me."

"Aw, come on. That's just a story," Sam said. "A myth, like the stories of the haints in Fearsome Hollow. Some little girl gets lost in the woods and comes home to find all the people in town … gone, vanished."

"Makes a good story, though, and I *do* like a good story," Charlie said. "And the little girl must have been like Tarzan, except instead of being raised by chimps in the jungle, she was raised by chipmunks in the woods."

"Maybe she's like the blue people of Troublesome Creek," Malachi said. "Everybody thought they didn't exist, even though lots of people claimed sightings over the years. Then lo and behold, it was true."

As a matter of fact, Sam had been telling Rusty about the blue people a three-week lifetime ago, sitting on the porch looking at the stars on a spring evening. How there were rumors, stories, "myths" about people whose skin was as blue as an ink stain on a shirt living in the mountains around Troublesome Creek near Hazard. Then when Sam was a sophomore in high school, they "came out of the closet," appeared. And a hematologist from the University of Kentucky figured out the mystery of their blue skin.

Because of isolation and inbreeding, seven generations of the Fugate family had been suffering from a rare genetic disorder that was easily cured. Left untreated, it turned their skin blue.

"So you think the three of us really did meet the Gideon Witch when we were on a first-grade field trip?" Sam said.

"Why not?" Charlie said. "We were seven, so that would have been 1970. When did Gideon become a ghost town?"

"About 1900, no, a few years before that," Sam said.

"In ... *1895*, maybe," Malachi said, in an odd tone of voice.

"So she'd have been old as dirt, but it is *possible*," Charlie said. "If she lived up in the woods somewhere nearby ... and suddenly there's all this commotion, school busses and shrieking children."

"So she came to have a look-see, and ran into the three of us in the woods," Sam suggested.

"No, she *found* the three of us in the mist," Charlie said. "It was so thick, I put my hand up and I really couldn't see it right there in front of my face. I never would have found my way back ... and then she was there."

Charlie reached into her purse again and pulled out a rock, round and brown and ugly, but on the other side were crystals.

"And she gave me this."

When Sam saw it, she gasped.

"I have one just like that," she cried. "I never knew where I got it. I just thought it was pretty, so I kept it. It's in a bowl with a bunch of seashells from the time we went to Florida." She reached out and took the rock from Charlie, turned it over in her hand. "I'd be willing to bet if I brought my rock and put it with this one, it'd fit. It's a geode, broken in half."

"And the halves broken in half," Malachi said. "Quarters."

"Seriously. You have a rock like this, too?"

"*Had* one. It was in my pack when the Humvee hit that IED."

He got a faraway look in his eyes and Sam was suddenly sorry she'd asked. He had come back to them while they were talking about the picture. His eyes had come to life, he was present, there. But at the mention of his rock, she watched the shutters slam shut on all the windows in his soul, the doors bang closed, the latches whack into place.

Malachi Tackett had left the building.

Chapter Fifteen

Charlie watched Malachi withdraw into himself, reminded her of a turtle retracting its head and legs into the shell and closing up the bottom. Clearly, there was some awful memory associated with that rock — not as they'd gotten it when they were children, but since then, something to do with fighting and blood and soldiers and war.

She reached out instinctively to grab him, to bring him back. Scrambling, she said, "Malachi, you seem to remember this day better than Sam and I do. What did that woman say to us?"

She shot a glance at Sam, who took the handoff like she'd been a football star instead of basketball.

"You were standing there while she was yelling at Charlie. What'd she say?"

"She wasn't yelling," he said softly. And Charlie was gratified to see that Malachi was fighting his way back. That he didn't want to stay where some terrible memory had taken him.

"Not yelling? Sure seemed like yelling to me — didn't it to you, Sam?"

"I'm still not sure I even *saw* a woman."

"It was yelling in intensity," Malachi said and they watched the light begin to grow in his eyes, like his soul had a dimmer switch and he was carefully dialing it back up. "She was intense, so maybe on the receiving end it felt like yelling."

"But she wasn't angry," Sam said, and there was recognition in her eyes like she'd just figured that part out. "I do remember her! Butt ugly. Breath that'd gag a maggot. I remember." Sam was thrilled. "I actually saw the Gideon Witch. How cool is that! She was intense, alright, but I think you're right, Malachi — she wasn't mad."

"Maybe not …" Charlie struggled to call up the images. "In fact, it sounded more like … pleading than yelling."

"She didn't want you to forget," Malachi said. "That's what the rocks were about. Not forgetting."

And then Charlie did remember.

THE OLD WOMAN smells like wood smoke and old dirt, like clothes that have needed washing so long they are stiff. Her breath over the stumps of her rotten teeth smells worse than Badger's breath, and his doggie breath is the worst.

"You hadn't ought to have come up here like you done," she says. "It lets me and mine be because we done right by it, but now it's marked you."

Charlie has no idea what the woman is talking about, cuts a glance at Malachi and Sam, who don't look like they know either. She wants to ask the woman to let go of her arm, but she is too frightened to speak.

"I run away! Got my nose all outa joint cause I got blamed when it was my little brother broke the jar. So I run away! Ten years old

and I run off into the woods crying, wasn't watching where I's going and got lost and it got dark and ..."

The old woman hasn't been looking at her, but she does now.

"... when I come back, they's all gone. Nary a soul left in all of Gideon. Wasn't nothing but the houses. No furniture. No clothes in the chifforobe or food in the kitchen. No cooking pots, no washtub. A mirror on the wall ... that's all, and the pegs my Daddy'd put in the wall by the door to hang coats on. Wasn't no coats, though. Everything was gone."

She finally lets go of Charlie's arm, and Charlie wants to rub where it's sore from her squeezing, but she doesn't, is afraid if she does the woman will grab her again. Maybe Charlie should run away while she has a chance. But run where? Back out there into the mist to get lost again? At least here, she's with Malachi and Sam.

An ancient drawstring bag hangs around the old woman's neck from a leather thong. With filthy fingers, she pulls open the bag and drops the contents out into the palm of her hand. It's a rock, and when she nudges the rock with her finger it falls apart and you can see it's one rock that'd been broken apart and had been stuck back together again.

"They was still there. Them people was still in Gideon for a time, you just couldn't see them, that's all. This here rock proves it."

She describes a trail that ran beside her house into the woods, the one she had taken the afternoon she ran away.

"I did love me rocks something fierce and my daddy was always getting pretty ones for me out of the creek when he went fishing. It was three days after everybody vanished. I's near crazy, hungry, scared to death all by myself, wandering around. And I come down that trail and one of the pieces of this here rock was laying in the dirt. It hadn't been there the day before."

She tells Charlie that she came back the next day, and there was another piece in the same spot. And another one the third day. Three pieces. But no more. She went back every day for a month looking for the final piece and found nothing.

"They's gone by then," she says. "My family, mama and my brothers and sisters and my daddy — all them people had been there for a few days, but then ... it took them."

She looks from Charlie to Sam and Malachi, who look as scared as Charlie feels.

"Its time's coming. Won't be long now. You three shouldn't a come up here, running around, laughing and having fun, giggling and the like. Making it want. Don't you never come back."

She gets down in their faces.

"Can you remember that?"

They don't reply, just look at her.

She shakes her head, looks down at the rocks in the palm of her hand and seems to make a decision. Grabbing Charlie's hand this time, she turns it over and drops one of the rocks into it. She does the same with Sam and Malachi.

"These here are to remind you, so you don't forget. Years can take away your memories, but ever time you see these rocks, you remember: Don't you never come back here again. Not all three of you. Hear?"

And while they're standing there gaping at her, she turns and is gone, vanishes in the mist. The three don't even have time to be surprised because the mist sort of ... goes with her. It doesn't flow back up the mountain. It's like fog clearing.

It clears and the three of them are standing beside the oak tree where Charlie had been when the mist came.

WHEN CHARLIE FINISHED THE STORY, they sat together in silence. She turned the rock over and over in her hand. A memory rock.

"I saw the picture, remembered that day and I had to wonder." Charlie was fumbling for words now. "I mean ... is there some connection?" She didn't have to say "to the Jabberwock" for them to know what she was talking about. "I mean, Gideon *vanished*."

"Did it really?" Malachi said.

"How could that be a hoax?" Sam asked. "The ghost town is still there. At least I guess, it's not like I've been out to Fearsome Hollow to check."

"Just because there are abandoned buildings doesn't mean the people in them vanished in a puff of smoke overnight," Malachi points out, "and left a ten-year-old kid alone in the woods. There are abandoned coal camps all over these mountains."

"Gideon's not like the others, though," Charlie said. Coal camps were built by the mining companies to house the miners who dug the black rock out of the ground. The structures were slapped together quick and cheap. "The buildings in coal camps started falling apart when there were still people living in them, miners were constantly having to fix leaking roofs and …"

"And yet Gideon is still there more than a hundred years later," Sam said, understanding. "The buildings are crumbling, but I bet they're in no worse shape now than they were when they were built. How can that be?"

"It's almost like time there … is different." Now it's Malachi who's struggling to find words. "Doesn't work right in Gideon."

Charlie felt the bottom drop out of her stomach.

"It didn't the day we were there, either." She looked from one to the other before she continued. "We all agree we were lost in the mist for hours — right?"

"Yeah," Malachi said.

"Absolutely. It seemed like we were gone forever."

"Actually, we weren't even gone the length of a single song."

"What are you're talking about?" Sam asked.

"When I saw you below me, staring at the mist coming down the mountainside, I had turned to look at you because of the song. Cotton-Eyed Joe. The band was playing it and it was one of my all-time favorite songs and I wanted to hear it."

Suddenly, Charlie didn't seem to have enough air to keep talking, the implications of what she was proposing were becoming frighteningly clear.

"… you wanted to hear it, and …?" Sam prodded.

"When she left us standing beside that oak tree, I could hear the music again and the band was just wrapping up a song. Cotton-Eyed Joe."

"They played it twice. I don't get your point."

"I do," Malachi said. "They only played it *one time* … and we left and came back during that one time.

"But we were gone for—" Sam began, sputtering.

"Think about it," Malachi said. "Reason it out. If we had been gone as long as we all remember being gone, wandering around lost, calling out — they'd have missed us."

Sam got it.

"If we hadn't been there when they started counting noses to load up the buses, they'd have sent out the Royal Canadian Mounted Police with bloodhounds to find us."

"We made it back to school in time for me to catch the school bus home," Malachi said. "Or my mother would have been the lead bloodhound."

"How can that be? How can—?"

Charlie didn't finish. At that moment the door opened and in strode two peas in a pod. Didn't knock. Apparently, Raylynn had told the Tungate brothers where to find them and from the looks on their faces, whatever they'd come to say couldn't wait.

"Abner's gone," Roscoe said. Or maybe it was Harry. Charlie never could keep the two of them straight.

"Abner …?"

"Abner Riley," said the other Tungate, and she thought he was the butcher, which would make the first one Harry. "Lives up Fearsome Hollow."

Fearsome Hollow.

"It ain't just that he's gone," said Roscoe. "It's *how* he's gone."

Then Harry Tungate told them his story.

Chapter Sixteen

E.J. didn't usually make "house calls" for dogs. You could bring a dog or cat into his office — or a goat or a sheep, for that matter. But bigger farm animals, he tended to on the farm. Judd lived on Sims Lane on the other side of Hollow Tree Ridge from Route 17 South. E.J. hadn't been out to Judd's farm since Judd's milk cow, a big Holstein with the most sour disposition of any cow E.J.'d ever met, was having trouble calving. He'd gone to the farm so he and Judd could pull the calf. Cows were large animals and gentle to a fault — which was a very good thing. E.J. had always thought that if they had ever sent a spy to the stockyards to see what happened to all their friends who left the farm and never returned, they could band together and do some serious damage. A Holstein weighed 1,500 to 2,000 pounds — about the size of the white rhino at the Louisville Zoo. Judd's Clementine had tried to mash E.J. up against the wall of the stall twice before they ever got that calf out of her.

The last time he had seen Buster was for that infected toenail. Part of Raylynn's job was to keep track of his patients' vaccinations and send out reminders to folks when the shots came due. He hadn't asked her, she'd been busy when he left, but he was sure she'd sent one to Judd months ago. But Judd's wife Mildred had died a year and a half ago, and he hadn't been firing on all cylinders in a long time.

That was part of the reason E.J. had dropped everything to go out to Judd's — because he felt bad that they hadn't followed up with him on Buster's shots, knowing he was likely to forget about it.

It wasn't like E.J. believed the dog had rabies. Just missing a booster didn't preordain infection. There were half a dozen reasons why a dog would stop eating his kibble, but the eating rocks part was concerning. E.J. would bet the behavior was linked to Mildred's death, and to Judd's subsequent inattention. Eating inanimate objects was usually a sign of stress and insecurity. But the behavior itself was concerning because chewing rocks was dangerous to a dog's mouth and teeth. Sharp edges could cut their gums and tongue, crunching could break teeth. And swallowing rocks could be deadly — an intestinal blockage or choking. It was also possible that Buster's diet was off — that he was trying to get calcium, magnesium or some other vitamin or mineral he wasn't getting in sufficient quantities.

Those were matters that needed to be addressed.

Killing the chicken, though … E.J. wasn't overly concerned about that. The dog was just being a dog. Even though humans believed they could train dogs out of innate behaviors just because humans found them upsetting, the results were usually mixed. He'd have to talk to Judd about the incident — had the chicken made a sudden movement, odd sound? Or was it possible Buster was only playing and because he was so big — Lenny in *Of Mice and Men,* "I done a bad thing, George."

The real bottom-line reason why E.J. was flying down Gallagher Station Road to the Perkins farm was that it was an excuse to get out of the office — a really good excuse — and he had to get out of there for a while or he would lose it in front of Sam or Raylynn or one of his "patients."

E.J. burped out a bleat of laughter. Never in more than a decade of veterinary practice had he given a moment's thought to his patients' opinion of him.

Bummer that Mrs. Throckmorton's Persian thinks I'm socially awkward.

I hate it that Billy Wainwright's basset hound is offended by my bad breath.

The Jabberwock.

"That's a nonsense word," he said out loud. "The whole thing is crazy, it's …"

Every day since the morning he had looked up to find Charlie Ryan — McClintock — in his office with a daughter in need of stitches, he had believed it would be over *soon.* Oh, not right away — gone in a couple of hours like other folks said it'd be. It'd take a few days, sure, maybe even a week, but eventually the crazy storm that had blown it into the county would come roaring back and blow it out again. And that's what it had to be — a storm. Okay, not exactly a "storm," but some weird meteorological phenomenon, something you didn't understand, maybe something nobody would ever understand, would spend years trying to figure out, but something real, tangible, a thing that happened and then unhappened for some kind of logical reason.

Because if it wasn't, if the Jabberwock didn't blow into the county on the heels of the wailing wind of that crazy storm two weeks ago ... what in the name of holy God was it?

E.J. turned his van, the one he'd used to take the odd assortment of humanity out to see the Jabberwock at the county line for the first time, off Gallagher Station Road and onto Sims Lane. Judd Perkins' farm was about a mile down, on the right. He looked at his gasoline gauge. He had had the presence of mind and the forethought that most other people had not — had filled up the tanks on both his van and his car the morning after ... Abby ... exploded.

Like every other farm in Nowhere County, Judd's farm was sandwiched in between mountains. His land stretched out on both sides of a nameless little creek that meandered down the hollow and his farm meandered, too. He had a small frame house that had once had beautiful roses growing along the fence that encircled the yard. The roses had been Mildred's and E.J. wasn't surprised to see that they hadn't been pruned, probably needed rose food and insecticide. Without Mildred ...

A gravel lane wound a quarter of a mile beside the creek to the house and E.J. pulled his van down it and into Judd's driveway. Judd's pickup wasn't in sight, and then E.J. remembered that it, like so many other vehicles, had been gobbled up by the Jabberwock.

The farm buildings were behind the house in the narrow strip of flat land where Judd grew a good-sized patch of tobacco and an assortment of vegetables, and kept a small herd of beef cattle and the lone milk cow — and perhaps her calf was still around. Oh, and there were chickens — free range, which had gotten one of their number killed in the past few hours. As he recalled, there were also geese, a couple of goats because Mildred had liked to make goat cheese, and a herd of sheep that provided mutton and lamb for their table.

E.J. got out of the van and walked in the open gate, up the sidewalk to the small concrete porch. There was a grape arbor on one side of the front lawn, and an Amish stand-up swing in the shade of the oak tree in the front yard. He knocked on the door. Nobody answered. He knocked again. Judd was probably out back tending to the livestock. Or in one of the barns. E.J. stepped off the porch and went around the side of the house, expecting to see Judd out in the farmyard behind the house. He wasn't there. Neither was Buster.

Judd was home, though. His farm truck was parked under a sycamore tree — an ancient International Harvester, the kind that looked like it was about to fall apart … and twenty years from now would still look like it was about to fall apart.

E.J. headed out across the open area in the barnyard toward the closed barn door.

Chapter Seventeen

Charlie knew why the Tungate brothers had come to the clinic to find her, Sam and Malachi to tell them what'd happened to Harry at Abner Riley's house and to ask for their help to find him. It was because the three of them, along with Liam and E.J., had taken charge of the Middle of Nowhere on J-Day, kept the wheels on during the disaster, and she shuddered to think what it would have been like there if they hadn't. But the fallout from that was that many nowhere people now looked to them for continuing leadership, and dealing with the ongoing disaster the Jabberwock had created would most certainly be harder than organizing teams to hose the vomit off the Dollar General Store parking lot.

Charlie volunteered to drive them to Fearsome Hollow.

"You need to know, I've never been to Fearsome Hollow," she said.

"Yes, you have," Malachi corrected.

"Okay," she amended. "I mean I've never gone there on my own, on purpose."

He looked like he was about to correct her again, but

didn't. When their eyes met for a moment, she felt the fluttering of a memory — a campfire, laughter. The image was a moth, there and then gone again. He looked away and she got behind the wheel and checked the fuel gauge. Everybody in Nowhere County did that these days. Luckily, her mother's car was a Honda Legend and it had had a full tank of gas when she got here and she'd driven it fewer than twenty-five miles since.

Sam stayed behind because E.J. had not yet returned from wherever he had gone running off to right before noon. Charlie pulled out of the parking lot and headed east on County Road 278 E, known to locals as simply "Lexington Road." Fair enough. It did eventually end up there. When she glanced in the rearview mirror, the Tungate twins in the backseat looked like two halves of an Oreo cookie without the white stuff in the middle — or would have if they'd been black.

Black.

Stuart's face washed into her mind and she was shocked by the tears that sprang instantly into her eyes.

She has never dated a black man. In actual point of fact there'd been only a handful of African Americans in all of Nowhere County when she was growing up. Stuart McClintock's skin is a beautiful color dark, but not black-as-a-piece-of-coal dark.

She had met him in the elevator of the Hitchcock Building. They were alone, side by side, observing elevator etiquette, looking resolutely at the numbers slowly changing and not at each other. But no way could she miss how good-looking he was. His face was perfect, looked like it'd been molded from a statue in the public square in Rome. And his somewhere-way-north of six feet height made him a "presence," even in the subdued tones of his immaculate business suit.

The doors open on his floor and in front of them is a suite of offices: Sawyer, Cohen, Hampton, Levine, Blackledge, and McClintock, Attorneys at Law.

"Is it true that the more names there are on the door of a law office, the more the attorneys charge per hour?" She can't believe she's said it, had thought it and out her mouth the words fell. A horrible breach of elevator decorum.

He doesn't seem to mind, though. Smiles. A warm, friendly, disarming smile.

"Absolutely true, but it's in descending order," he says, his voice a pleasant baritone. "The first name gets to charge a gazillion dollars an hour, the second name only half a gazillion. I'm Stuart McClintock." He extends his hand and she shakes it. "I get to charge a buck-two-ninety-eight."

That's how it starts.

After that chance encounter, Charlie goes way more than is necessary to the offices of her publisher in the Hitchcock Building, but after half a dozen visits, she gives up on ever "accidentally" running into him again.

When her phone rings a couple of weeks later, she instantly recognizes the baritone.

"Remember me, the pitiful little attorney at the end of the name game?" There was nothing either pitiful or little about Stuart McClintock. "I tracked you down through the receptionist at Hanover Publishing. She's become my new best friend, and she could get fired for giving me your number so please take pity on her. I had to give her a coupon for full legal services for the rest of her life as a bribe." He took a breath. "The thing is, if I got frequent flyer miles for riding up and down in an elevator hoping to run into you, I could exchange them for a ticket to Barundi. Will you have dinner with me tomorrow night?"

Light and airy and funny. That first dinner, she had been fascinated by his hands, told him he had beautiful hands, long slender fingers. She mostly knew coal miners, she said. Their hands were imbedded with a black that'd never wash off, were scarred or missing key digits.

And she'd been gratified by his response when he discovered that Charlie Ryan was the famous C.R.R. Underhill. He loved the books, didn't care if they were for children, he'd read them all.

Oh, they dated for several months before running off to Acapulco to get married, but he had her as soon as he correctly guessed the origin of her pen name. When he did, he quoted the One Ring spiel — "three rings for the elven kings under the sky, seven for the dwarf lords in their halls of stone, nine for mortal men doomed to die, one for the Dark Lord on his dark throne in the Land of Mordor where the shadows lie."

They finished the last part in unison. "One ring to rule them all, one ring to find them, one ring to bring them all and in the darkness bind them." He'd dropped his voice then, made it deep and sinister. "In the land of Mordor where the shadows lie."

She knew at that moment that he was the man she'd been waiting for her whole life.

"ARE YOU ALRIGHT?" Malachi was sitting in the front seat beside her and had seen the tears.

"No, not really, but I'm getting there." She gave him a wan smile. "Okay, trying to get there."

"I'd go down Byrne Lane, I's you," said Roscoe from the backseat and she obediently passed up where she'd intended to turn off onto Pebble Bottom Road. She'd forgotten that was a thing here. Since the roads meandered around the mountains, twisted and turned and tangled, getting from point A to point B involved multiple decisions about which roads to take. And people got territorial — *their* way to get from Bugtussle Hollow to Bennetville — by way of Bat Cave Road, Chimney Rock Pike and Elkhorn Road to County Road 278, then Barber's Mill Road south to Cicada Springs Road — was the *best* way, and men would get into fist fights about it.

PETE RUTHERFORD HADN'T REALLY INTENDED to start his project. It had sort of happened to him. Over the course of thirty-five years as a mailman — no a mail *carrier*, you wasn't allowed to be a "man" at anything anymore — Pete had been up and down every road, lane, dirt track, cattle run, logging road and deer trail in Nowhere County. And when he'd get assigned a new route, he'd make notes for himself so's he wouldn't get lost. Probably weren't half a dozen road name signs still on posts in the whole county. Most places, even the posts was gone and if there happened to be — praise God — an actual sign, it was so full of bullet holes you couldn't read it anyway. So he had scraps of paper that said what road forked off of what other road, added in what creek was always swollen after a rain, so he wouldn't get stuck, things like that.

After he'd retired, he had come across a box that had all them scraps of paper in them, little maps and drawings and instructions. And he'd thought maybe he'd just draw himself a map of Nower County.

That's what it'd been in the beginning. Just a little map. The ones issued by the state only included about three roads on them, and only one — Persimmon Ridge — of the half-dozen towns. None of the smaller roads were listed on state maps. He hadn't seen the map for 1995 yet. There'd been one in a rack at Mini Mart in Drayton County a couple of days before J-Day and he'd grabbed a copy and put it in his glove box, but hadn't looked at it yet. Kentucky maps became "official" on June 1 of every year, which this year had happened to be two days before J-Day and he'd had way bigger fish to fry since then than look at a map that never got anything right anyway.

The project Pete had started years ago had grown over time. He'd used a piece of poster board at first, but it wouldn't fit on just one. He eventually ended up drawing out small portions of the whole map on those. He'd been tinkering with it for a couple of years when he got the piece of canvas — like artists use to paint with oils or acrylics — only he ordered this piece special. It was ten feet across and eight feet from top to bottom. He hung it up on the wall in the living room. He moved the couch so he could get to all of it. Then he started to put the whole thing together there. Just a hobby. It was about the time he'd found out he had cancer and when he'd first started taking treatments. He hadn't felt good enough to leave the house, so he'd spend a little time every day drawing.

Now, when he looked at it, he was kinda awed at what it had become. If you work on anything a little bit every day for years, the result is usually pretty impressive and this map was.

It had every natural and man-made anything in the whole county. It was all there, labeled in his perfect penmanship. The creeks that fed into streams, swole up into rivers in the springtime and dried up into rock paths in the heat of summer. Every mountain, ridge, valley and hollow. The roads, of course — the names the post office had required on addressees, though the folks living on them roads might not have called them that.

From the Wiley Bridge, a historic covered bridge spanning the North Fork of the Rolling Fork River, to Route 15 which ran west of the Middle of Nowhere, connecting Drayton County in the south to Beaufort County in the north. Through Twig, where Roberta Callison ran a chicken farm, and Wiley, the home of poor old Willie

Cochran, missing both thumbs from a mining accident and who was the first fatality of the Jabberwock.

Pete looked from one landmark to another.

Bugtussle Hollow, where a cave in the limestone furnished a home to the bats that kept the mosquito population in Persimmon Ridge at bay, sitting in the shadow of Bishop Mountain with its stand of shagbark hickory trees on the southern slopes that turned an impossible bright golden yellow in the fall.

Ironwood Mountain, where the Scott's Ridge Overlook on the cliff face provided a panoramic view of the Rolling Fork River two hundred feet below.

Little McGuire Hollow, where a clan of red-headed, freckle-faced McGuires had lived for generations, and Solomon Hollow, home to Harry Tungate, Grace Tibbits and the Cawdreys, who'd given Abby Clayton a lift to the county line for her third ride on the Jabberwock.

Sugar Bowl Mountain, sitting just like a sugar bowl between Nates Creek Hollow and Harrow Woods west of Killarney cast a shadow over Turkey Neck Hollow, where the Tacketts lived high on the side of Gizzard Ridge.

And in much smaller print, Pete had put little "you are here" symbols like was on the sign in the Middle of Nowhere, and put the names of families he knew lived along the roads.

It was stunning in its detail, a work of art. And it was accurate.

Except it wasn't, of course.

Not in Fearsome Hollow, it wasn't. He didn't like looking at that part of the project. Roads and creeks and "You are Here's" were there, just like in every other part of the county. But the notes he'd used to place them had been erased and redone, and erased again so often the paper was worn thin and fragile. Because the mist … obscured things. No, it was more than that. Much as he was loath to admit it, Pete Rutherford would swear that things in Fearsome Hollow *moved around*. You couldn't make an accurate map of a place where sometimes a road was here, and other times …

❧

ROSCOE WAS WEARING a chambray shirt while Harry had on a University of Kentucky tee shirt. She was able to tell them apart now, though, after listening to Harry's story, watching his face as he told it, and she would never again mistake him for Roscoe.

Charlie had remembered Abner Riley from the nightmare of J-Day — he was unforgettable, with his tortured "harelip" speech and the jagged scar on his lip. She'd had to concentrate to keep from looking at it, made herself look into his eyes and she found there a kindness and … peace she hadn't seen in many people in her life.

She had never seen him again after that day, had no idea he lived in Fearsome Hollow. In truth, she had trouble believing anybody actually *lived* here. The stories about haints and all manner of other strange happenings … you could blow them off, sitting in the bright sunshine around a barbecue grill behind her mother's house beneath Little Bear Mountain. But *living* in Fearsome Hollow, in the midnight dark, with a keening wind … well, it was a hardy soul who could go with that and not worry about all the things that inevitably go bump in the night.

Gabe Stump Road ran alongside a nameless little stream that fed into Troublesome Creek, which formed the waterfall in Gideon. In lots of places in the mountains, this being one of them, there was only room enough between the inclines for the road and the stream bed, and sometimes the old railroad tracks that hadn't been used since miners dug coal out of the mountains with picks and shipped in on huge coal cars north to Andrew Carnegie's steel mills in Pennsylvania. The road and stream were nothing like the highway and the Rolling Fork River, but still they reminded Charlie uncomfortably of the night Abby had hauled her out to the county line and demanded she get rid of the Jabberwock so Abby could go to Lexington to—

"The mist." Just those two words. Harry spoke them from the back seat and Charlie turned to look where he pointed. High above them, blotting out the steep walls of the surrounding mountains was a puddle of white like cream on top of a bucket of milk. The mist was intimidating and foreboding even way up there.

"We're like to get a closer look at it than this before we leave Fearsome Hollow," Roscoe said.

Chapter Eighteen

E.J. noticed a pile of something that looked like feathers against the wall of the barn. It registered in the higher centers of his brain what it actually was a couple of seconds too late. Not just feathers. There were feet, webbed feet. A goose. The remains of a goose. A dead goose.

"What about the chicken?" Judd had asked when he called.

"What chicken?"

"The chicken Buster killed this morning."

The veterinarian seemed to think the thoughts slowly, rationally, absorbing the full meaning of each one. That's what it felt like, but in reality E.J. had thought through the whole process between one eye blink and the next and had reached the horrifying conclusion before he blinked again.

Buster had refused to drink from his dog dish.

Buster had been eating rocks and clods of dirt.

Buster had refused to look at Judd.

Buster had been walking funny, limping.

Buster had killed a chicken. And a goose.

... and Buster had missed his last rabies booster.

A big white dog came around the side of the barn then. It was shaking its head, yanking it to the right rhythmically, like it had something stuck on its snout and was trying to shake it off.

Yep, Buster was rabid alright.

The thought was dispassionate, clinical. A diagnosis based on the available data. The full realization of what that meant at that particular moment parked at the curb of time took another heartbeat to register.

Buster was huge, easily as big as a mountain lion. And right now, way more vicious than one.

E.J. froze, which turned out to be the right response, though he hadn't done it as an act of volition. He had been so shocked that his muscles were not responding to the signals he was sending to them to run.

Buster stood where he was, shaking his head. If he charged, he would kill E.J. instantly. Instantly, if the veterinarian were lucky. Because the attack would not be an instinctual animal response to food on the hoof, Buster might not go for the throat, the kill shot, right away. He would likely maul E.J. first, then kill him.

The eye was drawn to movement, and E.J. hadn't moved. It was possible Buster had not seen him. Yeah, right. Standing out in the middle of an empty barnyard, E.J. stuck out like a cherry red Mustang at a car show. But rabies did all manner of horrifying things to the brain. A not-exhaustive list included blindness. Though sight didn't provide a dog much information about the world, maybe Buster's vision had been impaired. It was equally possible that his primary senses, smell and hearing, weren't firing on all cylinders, either, but best not count on being dealt a royal flush. A dog's sense of smell was staggeringly superior to a human's, 10,000 to 100,000 times stronger. If it were sight instead of smell, what a human could see at one foot, a dog could see twenty miles away. A dog could hear a human heartbeat behind a closed door, and the heart that was currently jackhammering a hole in E.J.'s chest probably sounded like one, too.

He was standing downwind of the dog and the animal was not yet aware of him. He had a couple of seconds.

Without moving his head, E.J.'s eyes frantically raked the barnyard. Nothing that could be used as a weapon was in sight. No obvious place to escape that he could outrun the dog to. On the ground beside his foot was a rock about the size of his fist. He would not likely hold off a rabid 170-pound Great Pyrenees with a rock.

What he did next he did from pure instinct, though surely it had gone through some process of analysis, and a forming of intent that had merely been too fast for E.J. to follow. Bending at the knee, never taking his eyes off the dog that was still wagging its head from side to side, he knelt and picked up the rock.

Not anybody's definition of a jock in high school, E.J. had been too skinny and scrawny to play football and not tall enough for basketball. But he had played baseball. Left field. And, in the verbiage of major league baseball announcers, "he had an arm on him." When he drew back to throw, the motion caught the attention of the dog. It looked up, saw him.

E.J. threw the rock with all the force that his natural ability, spiked by the adrenaline rush of abject terror, could bring to bear. When it hit the tin shed about fifteen feet to the dog's right, it sounded like the retort of a Howitzer.

Bam!

The dog's massive head jerked in that direction and it leapt, primed to attack whatever had made the sound. At the same time, E.J. took off running for the barn. The dog would see him, see the movement. But it would be too absorbed in the sound it had heard to care. Or not. Either way, E.J. had a two-second head start on the dog and he never looked back.

Running faster than he'd ever have believed possible, E.J. tore out across an impossibly wide twenty-foot stretch of bare dirt toward the side door of the barn, slammed into it, grabbed the handle and yanked.

The door was latched on the inside.

WHEN BUSTER STUCK his snout through the hole in the side of the barn, Judd got his first look at the dog's eyes. Gone was the gentle intelligence.

He had commented to Mildred dozens of times that looking into Buster's brown eyes was like looking at marbles that didn't even have no black spot in the middle. She had finally dragged him and the dog over to the window and made him look at Buster's eyes in the bright sunlight, and sure enough, there was a black spot in the middle of what looked like — in bright sunlight at least — liquid caramel.

After that, Judd had always thought of the dog's eyes like that — even at night when all he could see were dark spots on white fur, he imagined he could see them caramel eyes with the sun twinkling in them.

Them eyes — well, he used the rest of his body, too — could make the dog look silly. He'd plop that big head on the floor on his front paws, while his huge back end was standing up and tail wagging and you could flat out see the amusement in his eyes.

He could look like he cared, like he was grieving right alongside Judd. After Millie passed, Judd would find himself wandering from one room of the house to another, not looking for anything, just wandering around and Buster was right there, one step behind him.

And there was times, in them first few weeks, that Judd would go down on one knee in front of the dog, wrap his arms around the animal's neck and sob into that mane of white fur. Buster would snuggle closer to him when he done that. Sometimes, he'd even put out his paw and … wasn't any other way to describe it, he'd pat Judd on the shoulder.

And Judd would swear, bring him a stack of Bibles and he'd put his hand on them and challenge God to strike him dead with a lightning bolt if he was lying — he'd swear Buster cried, too. He seen tears in them eyes, running down the fur on his snout and wasn't no other explanation for that except he was crying.

There was love in them eyes, intelligence, fun and—

All that was gone now. What Judd seen in the eyes of the dog that'd got most of his whole head through the opening was madness. Pure madness. Judd would never have thought such a thing was possible, had secretly dreaded the fact that the dog was not going to live as long as he was, that one of these days he was gonna have to take him in to E.J. and sit patting his head as he went to sleep. He had thought about it — wouldn't let himself go there often, but he'd thought about it and he was sure that he absolutely would not be able to stand it.

As he looked into the mad eyes of the crazed beast trying to dig into the barn to kill him, Judd knew that Buster wasn't in there anymore. Rabies had already killed Buster, and Judd would be glad to put an end to the suffering of his body if he could. He would put a bullet into the brain of that beast and be grateful the good Lord had give it to him to do.

But he couldn't put a bullet in the dog's brain now because he didn't have a rifle. Didn't have a weapon of any kind. Had grabbed at an old broom handle on the floor and beat on his snout to get him to back out of the hole. That'd drove him away for a moment, then he lunged again and the weight of him popped loose another one of the boards.

He could keep the dog out beyond the barn door with the latch — and all Judd's weight held against it. He couldn't whack at the dog with a broom handle and keep him from digging through the hole in the barn wall.

Looking around frantically, for anything to hit him with, anything to stick in the hole—

The whiskey barrel.

He'd got it at Maker's Mark Distillery in Marion County years ago, a big old white oak barrel. Before he cut it apart to make planters for Millie to put flowers in on both sides of the front walk, he'd leached the liquor out of it. Whiskey barrels only got used to make whiskey once. The making of whiskey required a brand new white oak barrel that was charred on the inside — he'd seen that part once when he was at a cooperage getting used staves for firewood and them barrels rolled down an assembly line and past this thing that squirted flames out into them, looked like a dragon.

After whiskey aged in the barrels for seven years, they couldn't be re-used, so the distillery sold them, knowing full well that you could go home, put water in them, seal them up and put them out in the hot sun and leach out a couple of quarts of whiskey that'd soaked into the wood. Same whiskey the distillery sold in bottles you could get without paying for the whiskey or the government tax.

He never had got around to cutting the barrel in two

before Millie got sick, so he'd just stuck the barrel in the barn.

Judd leapt to his feet, grabbed the barrel and wrestled it onto its side as Buster lunged at the hole again and broke a board clean off. He rolled the barrel up to the wall beside the hole and set it upright in front of the broken boards. The next time Buster lunged he ran into the oak of the barrel, musta hurt but he never cried out. Wasn't no way he was gonna break through that and heavy as it was, he wouldn't be moving it neither.

Then Buster was gone. Didn't even try again, stopped lunging and … yeah, and what?

Where did he go?

Judd leaned on the top of the barrel, and took two ragged deep breaths.

Bam!

Sounded like a rifle shot — but it wasn't a sharp enough crack for that. Seconds later, something slammed into the barn door and a voice cried out, "Judd!"

It was E.J.! *Out there with Buster.*

If Judd opened the door, the dog would get into the barn and kill them both.

Chapter Nineteen

Charlie couldn't help scanning the hillsides for the blotch of white that could settle down off the mountain on them like a blanket. Up among the trees, it just looked like ordinary creek mist, tattered and frayed, like it'd dissipate if you puffed a breeze at it.

The sky was blue and the sun was shining when Harry instructed them to pull over at the next house. He'd said Abner lived at 2433 Fog Bottom Lane, but there'd been no road sign to identify it when they'd turned off Gabe Stump Road, and there was no mailbox either and no house number on the house.

The front door of the house was standing open. But that was the only thing that fit the description Harry Tungate had given.

Harry and Roscoe got out of the car slowly and stood beside it gawking at the house, identical looks of confusion and fear stamped on their features.

"What ... what's happened here?"

"I thought you said Abner kept his place so neat ..."

"This ain't about Abner," Roscoe said, looking at

Harry. "This here's something else entirely. This here's …" He didn't finish, just gestured at the house and yard before them.

Abner Riley's house was nothing like the pristine little brick home Harry had seen only a few hours ago. It was a dilapidated old brick house that appeared to be still standing only because the brick walls hadn't caved in.

The roof had. It was sunken in a heap in the middle, had moss and greenery growing on the ancient roof tiles. The white paint was … well, if there'd been white paint, it was nowhere in evidence on the shutters or the trim. The wood was gray with age. The picket fence was only standing where it was attached to the gate. It was a tangled gnarl of ancient gray pickets lying in the mass of weeds that surrounded the house. There was no yard. Though the gate was gone, the sidewalk still stretched from the gate posts to the porch, through years' and years' worth of briars and brambles that narrowed the walkway so that you'd have to edge sideways to get through. The front door was hanging by one hinge. You could see in through it, in the light of the hole the roof collapse had created, where sunshine illuminated a shamble of interior overgrown by weeds and vines.

The house looked seventy-five, maybe a hundred years old. Maybe older.

"How could *this*" — Harry waved his hand around in a gesture that encompassed it all — "have happened since this morning?" His voice was breathy.

"Don't see no point in looking for Abner here," Roscoe said, but Harry started down the sidewalk anyway. "Don't you go in there or the roof's gonna fall in on you." Roscoe ignored him.

Charlie fell in behind Roscoe, with no intent but to get a better look at the building, certainly not to search the interior. When Roscoe stopped abruptly in front of her, she almost ran into him.

"Feel that?" His voice was tight with fear. "Feel the cold?"

And she did. A breeze was issuing out the hanging-by-a-hinge door, cool. Unnaturally cool.

That was singularly odd for a couple of reasons, the most important of which was that the wind wasn't blowing. The leaves on the tangle of vegetation were still.

Malachi came up behind her on the sidewalk.

"That's what you were talking about?" Malachi indicated the door and the chill.

"Yeah, but it was colder then. A crap-ton colder than it is now."

With his words, the temperature of the breeze seemed to drop.

"Let's get out of here." Harry turned and pushed Charlie along in front of him toward the car. She felt the wind then, behind her. Cold on her neck.

"Go on, now. Get in the car," Harry told her, looking back over his shoulder.

Malachi took Charlie's arm and pulled her along beside him, not dragging her but the next thing to it. He only let go of her to push her into the driver's seat, then hurried around the car to the passenger side. Harry and Roscoe dived one after the other into the backseat.

"Go on!" they urged in unison.

The wind was frigid now. Like the breath off a glacier.

Charlie slammed the door and looked at the house, saw that the cold was not a wind that touched the leaves of the vines, brambles and weeds. They remained still, but the cold breeze had been blowing strong enough to lift Charlie's hair off her neck before she got into the car.

"Don't turn around, just go on straight," Roscoe instructed her, "make for Frogtown Road."

Charlie pulled back onto the road that ran in front of Abner's house, fear shoving her foot so hard on the accelerator that gravel flew out behind the back tires.

And she imagined she could see her breath frosting in front of her as she drove.

~

WHAT REECE HAD the hardest time figuring out was what to put it in. And in the end, he decided not to put it in anything.

He had only spent a few summers working in the mines when he was a young man before they closed, and by that time they had progressed way past the point of using dynamite to blow coal out of the seam. A machine called a continuous miner now did the job dynamite had once done, faster and safer.

Reece'd learned what he knew about blasting from working for TCC, Talbot Coal Co., Inc., in West Virginia, a company that not only distorted the landscape but mangled the language used to describe what they did. TCC engaged in "mountaintop restructuring," their euphemism for strip mining, where they removed "overburden," their euphemism for all the mountaintop that wasn't coal. The amount of explosive necessary per cubic yard of overburden was called "the powder factor."

What they actually did, of course, was demolish the mountains and plow their remains off into the surrounding valleys. That, of course, leveled the land, totally screwing with the natural hydrology of the region. Given that streams flowed *down* mountains — no mountains, no downward flow, and suddenly surrounding rivers had no headwaters and no tributaries.

He'd read somewhere that the amount of rock blasted off the tops of mountains in West Virginia would cover the island of Manhattan in 250 feet of dirt.

Reece had become so disgusted with the whole process of strip mining that he'd flipped off his boss one afternoon, walked off the job and never went back. But after five years in the profession, Reece Tibbits knew his way around the most common explosive used in mining — ANFO, ammonium nitrate fuel oil. It was downright scary how easy it was to lay your hands on it because you could literally "make it out of leftover items in the garage." It was the explosive that McVeigh guy had used to blow up the federal building in Oklahoma City in April. Two ingredients — fertilizer and fuel oil. Reece had the better part of a fifty-pound bag of ammonium nitrate fertilizer in his garage — used the pellets on his vegetable garden. The Bashfords down the road used fuel oil for heat in the winter, had a big tank full of it, and they'd been visiting their daughter in Florida on J-Day.

In real-world blasting, you buried explosives in drilled holes, jammed tight so the explosion would rip apart the enclosure. But what if what you wanted to blow up didn't have solid sides? You couldn't drill a fire hole in a mirage. That thorny issue had kept him awake for two nights, before he realized he didn't need a fire hole to get the desired results.

Though lack of sleep had muddied his thinking, his logic was sound. The Jabberwock was some kind of ... force field ... It wasn't a solid anything, so blowing a hole in it would be merely blowing up air — right? The force you'd be blasting into had no visible, tangible sides, so it really didn't matter a fig newton what he put the explosive in.

So he had settled on just setting the barrel in which he had mixed the fuel oil and the ammonium nitrate pellets on a wooden pallet to which he had attached casters and a fifteen-foot length of rope. He had considered making an electrical detonator that he could set off with a garage door opener. But his mother had been a lifelong fan of the KISS principle — Keep It Simple, Stupid. So he fashioned a percussion detonator out of gunpowder that he could set off with a rifle shot. He was reasonably certain he could have triggered the explosion by firing a shot into the barrel itself, but a detonator left nothing to chance.

He was ready.

Chapter Twenty

With his shoulder jammed against the door, Judd unlatched it and let it open just enough for him to reach around it and grab E.J.'s arm to pull him inside. As he did, E.J. screamed. Buster had bitten into his leg and was pulling back the other direction. Judd yanked E.J.'s arm with all his strength, and with the momentum of E.J. lunging forward, the top part of his body fell through the small opening between the door and the jamb. He hit the dirt on his shoulder, but his legs were still outside the door, and Buster was attacking his calf with a fury.

Judd was wearing heavy rubber work boots. They'd protect him against …

He drew back his foot and kicked Buster in the snout as hard as he could, right in the nose, and blood spewed out of it. The dog didn't flinch, obviously felt no pain, but the force of the blow did knock him backwards off balance and he let go of E.J.'s leg, staggered sideways a little, wasn't steady on his feet.

Holding onto the door with his right hand, Judd grabbed a handful of E.J.'s shirt with his left. Judd was a brute, thick and muscled, but even he was surprised at the adrenaline-fueled strength that enabled him to yank E.J. through the doorway opening. He literally threw him into the room and then tried to close the door behind him.

Buster lunged at it before Judd could get it shut, hit it with such force it opened enough for the dog to insert his snout and front paws, snarling and growling, pawing at the dirt with his claws.

Judd's boots slid in the dirt and Buster's whole head came through the opening. Judd kicked again, caught Buster this time in the eye and the dog lifted his head up so he could bite into the boot. That shifted his weight backward and Judd again threw all his weight against the door, digging his boots into the dirt for traction.

The opening between the door and the jamb closed enough that Buster's huge head would no longer fit through it, but his snout was still jammed into the opening and his front paws clawed the dirt.

Only then did Judd see that E.J. was beside him, shoving with him at the door to close it.

Judd kicked as hard as he could at one of Buster's paws, had thought about slamming his boot down on it but clearly the dog felt no pain. The blow knocked the paw backward, he and E.J. shoved the door closed another inch and suddenly the dog removed his snout and remaining paw and the door slammed shut. Judd engaged the latch, turned with his back leaning against the door and braced his feet as the force of Buster jumping at the door rattled the latch and the hinges.

Bam!

Buster hit the door.

Bam!

He hit it again and the force of the blow jarred Judd and E.J. forward. But the door held.

Judd looked down at E.J.'s leg. Blood was gushing out of it. Buster had bitten his left calf, got the meat firm in his teeth and yanked. The wound was so gory, Judd couldn't tell for sure, but it looked like the dog had bitten a hunk of E.J.'s leg out of it.

Bam!

The dog hit the door again, but with both Judd and E.J. leaning against it, the door held. The men tensed, awaiting the *bam* of Buster's next lunge. But it didn't come. Panting, neither said anything, just kept their backs firm against the door. Waiting. They could hear the dog snarling.

"What's he doing?" E.J. asked, his voice breathy with pain. Judd turned and looked through a crack between the slats of the door. He could see Buster, ripping at the body of the goose he'd killed, tearing it apart, snarling and barking.

Buster had given up on the door, at least for the moment.

E.J. began to slide down the door, his legs giving way under him. With Buster lunging at the door, Judd had had all his attention focused on keeping the door closed. Now, he stepped away from it and picked up a shovel off the floor, the one he used to muck the cow dung out of the barn. He turned the shovel upside down and jammed the business end of it into the two-inch-wide space under the door, like a door stop. By itself, it wouldn't hold the door closed, but it would help.

Then Judd knelt on one knee beside E.J., who was sitting with his back against the door, his legs splayed out in front of him. E.J. didn't look right. He wasn't wearing his glasses. Must have gotten knocked off.

"What are you doing here?"

"I tried to call. Buster missed his rabies booster."

Judd thought, "Ya think?" but didn't say it. Instead he said, "I need to see to that leg."

"Water. You got any water?" E.J. was leaned over, trying to get a good look at the wound.

Judd looked around, his eye falling on a wooden bucket. There was only about six inches of water in it.

"It's filthy."

"Doesn't matter. It'll help to wash away …" He didn't have to finish.

Judd got the bucket and set it down beside E.J., who was instructing him to "use my tie for a tourniquet."

Judd had trouble getting the knot undone. His hands were shaking. E.J. reached up one hand, grabbed the knot and slid it halfway down to loosen it and Judd pulled it the rest of the way. When he started to wrap it around E.J.'s calf, E.J. said, "No, I'll do it. You stay away."

"You saying I can get … *it* … from touching your blood."

"No, but Buster's saliva … just keep back."

Judd felt helpless, but did as E.J. instructed. E.J. wrapped the tie twice around his leg just below the knee and tied it.

"Get me a stick."

Judd looked around, couldn't find anything he could use, then spotted a piece of wood about six inches long that Buster had torn loose out of the hole in the wall of the barn. He handed it to E.J., who wrapped the tie around it and then twisted it to tighten the tourniquet.

"Now the water."

Judd poured water over the wound. In the instant the blood was washed away, Judd caught sight of it. There were two huge gashes that ran down E.J.'s calf, eight or so inches long, all the way to his ankle. And a hole, in the meat of the back of his calf, a ragged …

Judd felt bile rise up in the back of his throat but he swallowed it back. Buster had bitten a chunk out of the back of E.J.'s calf, pieces of skin and tissue were dangling from it. Then the blood rushed back in and the hole was gone.

"Hold it," E.J. said, indicating the piece of bloody wood. Judd took hold of it. "Tighter." Judd twisted it, like the spigot on a garden hose, and watched the blood flow instantly diminish.

Then all the strength went out of E.J. and he collapsed back against the door, panting, his face the color of a bedsheet and covered in a thick sheen of sweat.

"Are you … wearing … a tee shirt?" E.J. was forcing the words out between teeth clamped shut to keep from screaming in pain.

"Yeah, sure."

"Take it off … use it for a bandage."

Judd yanked his chambray work shirt open without unbuttoning it, the buttons pinging off the door like shrapnel. He pulled it off and tossed it aside, then pulled off his tee shirt, revealing his big round belly and — he'd always been self-conscious about it — an outie navel that protruded so far it was probably a hernia.

"What do I do with the tee shirt?"

In gasped words and half sentences, E.J. told Judd how to rip strips of fabric off his shirt and then ball up a big piece of the tee shirt.

"There … put it there … in the … hole," E.J. said, and Judd did as he was directed, jammed the wadded-up cloth into the hole, then wrapped the strips of fabric around and around it to hold it in place.

"My belt." E.J. nodded toward the leather belt around his waist. It was thin, only about an inch wide. "Get it."

NINIE HAMMON

Judd unfastened the belt and slid it out of the belt loops.

"You got a knife?"

Judd fumbled in his pocket and pulled out a worn, well-used pocketknife.

"We're going to replace the tie with the belt and when we get it tight enough, I need you to poke holes in the leather so we can fasten it in place. Won't have to hold it like the piece of wood."

"Don't I got to release it, I mean aren't you supposed to—?"

"No!" E.J. barked. "Two hours. No muscle damage in two hours. Six hours and … amputate. I'd rather not bleed to death."

Judd did as he was instructed, wrapped the belt, let E.J. pull it as tight as he thought it should be, then poked a hole there and they fasted the tourniquet in place with the belt buckle. Then E.J. told Judd to release the tie tourniquet, and use the tie to wrap around the wound along with the pieces of fabric to hold the pressure bandage.

Once the tourniquet and bandages were in place, E.J. shoved Judd out of the way and vomited, heaved and gagged, then collapsed back against the door, panting. Judd got up and used a hoe to scoop up the vomit, dumped it in a corner and covered it with hay. He could still smell it, though, and had to fight his own gag reflex as he knelt back beside E.J.

The younger man finally opened his eyes, still panting.

"He got me good," he said.

"Yeah. You gonna have to take them shots in the stomach."

"They're not given in the stomach. That's a myth. And I won't be taking them anyway."

"Why not?"

130

"I don't have any. I don't keep human PEP — post-exposure prophylaxis — in my office. You get that at a doctor's office. I'm a vet, remember."

"But you've been vaccinated — right?"

E.J. just looked at him.

Chapter Twenty-One

Charlie hadn't driven half a mile from Abner's house when she rounded a corner and mist sat on the road ahead of them. Almost like it'd been waiting for them.

She braked, slowing, reluctant to drive into it, though it seemed ephemeral and gauzy — she could see the road ahead beyond it.

"Stop!" Harry said. "Turn around."

She stopped, reached to put the car in reverse.

"It's coming," Malachi said, and she looked up to see the mist gliding toward the car like fog rolling in off the sea. It swallowed the car and as soon as it did, Charlie could no longer see through it. It was a solid white mass.

"Ain't never seen the mist this thick," Harry said. A statement of fact with no indication of emotion in it whatsoever. Charlie knew it had taken a heroic act of will to seine the scared out of the words.

White … except there seemed to be shadows in it that shimmered with black light. Black light was impossible, but they'd all seen it before. When they rode the Jabberwock they'd been blinded by flashes of black light that sparkled like glitter. More and more shadows formed out of the nothingness of the mist, twinkling black shapes so obscured it was impossible to tell what they were. All that was discernible was that they were different sizes, some as small as a dog, others four or five feet tall. Their shapes seemed to change but maybe that was just the swirling of the mist, but the sizes remained the same. The shapes glided through the air, floating just far enough away so you couldn't make out details.

"Do you see …?" Charlie was surprised she had the air to speak.

"The shapes — yeah," Malachi said.

Even though the mist was pure white, it was so thick it blocked the sunlight and the interior of the car had grown darker and darker until the reflection of white off faces was all you could make out.

"What are they?"

"The haints," said one of the Tungates. Charlie didn't know which one.

"What do they want? Why—?"

Whispers.

Charlie jerked her head toward her window. Somebody out there had said …

"What?" Roscoe asked from the backseat.

"You don't hear it?"

"Hear what?" Harry asked.

"I hear it," Malachi said and when she turned to look at him the shadows on the planes of his face gave it a sinister look. "Whispering, like people talking in the next room and you can't quite hear what they're saying."

"I hear it," said Roscoe. Harry said nothing. "I can't make it out, though, the words, can't—"

"I don't want to know what the words are," Harry said.

Charlie made a connection. "Remember the whispering we heard that day we were lost in the mist?"

"I just remember the voices sounded like other children to me. I thought I was hearing the kids from down below."

There was a cry then. An otherworldly wail that was so chilling Charlie couldn't draw in a breath. It seemed to be some distance away. There was another then, closer. And another. It sounded something like distorted crying, a crude approximation of sobbing. Like the baby dolls she and Sam used to play with — when you moved them a certain way they'd let out a *waaahhh* sound. The sound grew louder, but somehow didn't drown out the whispers, the almost-words that seemed like different voices speaking urgently, like what they were trying to say was important.

"Did you hear crying that day?"

"Yeah, *I was crying.* Sam was, too, but I didn't hear her."

The wailing grew more plaintive, sorrowful, but Charlie sensed no genuine sadness. Like the heartbroken, inconsolable sobbing that Merrie could turn on and off like a spigot. And the dark shapes got closer, their black light sparkling, twinkling, not close enough to see but only barely obscured by the puffy white of the mist. They began to circle the car, just out of sight, making that pitiful wailing sound, or maybe something else was making the sound and they were whispering. The twinkling became flashes of light, the shapes floating around and around the car, strobes of light that left an afterimage like a flash of lightning.

The whispers became more and more urgent, then began to change into grumbles. Angry grumbles, like whoever or *whatever* was whispering was mad that nobody understood the words.

The tone of the sobbing changed, too, no longer

despairing and forlorn. Now, there was an element of anger in it, too, like the crying might transform into shouting. Yelling.

Something thumped on the back of the car. Charlie squeaked out a pitiful sound, not even strong enough to call a scream. The men looked around, their eyes huge.

"What was that?" she asked.

Useless question.

"A thing that goes bump in the night, only it's broad daylight," Malachi said.

Then the car ... moved. Charlie could feel it. Her eyes snapped from one to the other of the men in the car and didn't have to ask if they felt it, too.

There was a small creaking sound as the weight of the car began to lift up off the shocks, which were just about bottomed out with the load of passengers the car was carrying.

Then the car began to move forward.

Charlie slammed her foot down on the brake to stop the movement. But it did no good because the wheels weren't turning. The car wasn't *rolling* forward, but it definitely was moving forward.

"I bet it ain't far up here to the cut," Harry said.

"The cut?" Malachi asked.

"Abner warned me about it, said that hard rain we got the second week of May, the creek come up, took a chunk out of one side of the road. You got to be careful not to drive right off into it." He paused. "Creek's down now ... you'd drop thirty feet."

They exchanged horrified looks.

"Everybody got their seatbelts fastened?" Malachi asked.

Somehow, Charlie didn't think seatbelts would be any protection in this circumstance.

THIS WAS NOT the first time in his life that Elijah Hamilton, Doctor of *Veterinary* Medicine, had been bitten by an animal. He had no idea how many times. He'd never kept track. Cats, dogs. A horse bit him once and broke his finger. Roger Henderson in Crawford County raised alpacas and one of them came very close to biting off E.J.'s ear. All manner of beasts and fowl, both domestic and exotic. An animal bite was, after all, what had convinced him to become a vet in the first place. It had not been the savaging of a rabid Great Pyrenees the size of a cougar. It had been a mouse. A white mouse.

He'd begged, pleaded, whined, maybe even wailed, until his parents finally gave in and allowed him to purchase a mouse from the pet store on Harrodsburg Road in Lexington. He routinely hung out in the pet store. His father went to a weekly Alcoholics Anonymous meeting — steadfastly earning chips year after year — in the basement of the church across the street. E.J. always tagged along so he could go to the pet store and wander among the cages of exotic birds and reptiles, as well as yapping puppies and big-eyed, please-take-me-home kittens. E.J.'d never been allowed to have a cat or dog because his mother was allergic. Ten minutes in the presence of any creature with fur and his mother's eyes swelled shut.

It was during one of his visits to the pet store that he'd met Herman. Herman was a white mouse. One of a whole herd of them. He'd asked the owner of the pet store at the time if "herd" was the collective noun for mice and the man had just looked at him. But he knew it couldn't be something like school, or flock or swarm — nothing as weird as gang or murder, and he wanted to know what to call them. The mice lived in a big cage at the back of the store. E.J. suspected, though he never asked because he absolutely did not want to know, that the pet store provided lab mice to the University of Kentucky for all manner of medical research.

The first time E.J. pecked on the side of the glass enclosure, Herman came running, put his little pink paws on the glass, his wiggly little nose sniffing as if he could really smell E.J. on the other side. E.J. got down nose-to-nose with the little beastie, looking into his tiny marble eyes.

That was not a particularly significant encounter, but the next time E.J. went into the store, Herman disengaged himself from the group of mice by the food bowl and came running to the glass where E.J. was tapping. He thought it was the same mouse as before. It was hard to tell one white mouse from another in a glass cage with several dozen. He did note, this time, that this particular little mouse had a black spot in the center of his front left paw.

When E.J. returned to the store the next week, he went directly to the glass enclosure of white mice and one of them peeled away from the pack and came running to the glass. When he put his paws up on the glass, E.J. saw the little black spot.

That's when he'd started browbeating his parents to let him have Herman as a pet. It took weeks, and every time E.J. returned to the store, he was afraid Herman wouldn't be among the mice in the cage, and the thought of the cute little dude with the wiggly nose and marble eyes being dissected by some first-year biology student turned his stomach.

His parents finally gave in, his father accompanied him into the store to purchase the little creature and E.J. carried him home in the tiny cage the pet store owner had provided. E.J. took the little mouse into the bathroom, the smallest room in the house where there was nowhere for him to run or hide, and lifted the warm little mouse out of the cage.

Herman wiggled his nose at E.J. And then bit him.

The mouse sunk its tiny sharp teeth into the end of E.J.'s thumb and a drop of blood showed there instantly. E.J. leapt back and dropped the little creature into the sink, where the sides were too steep and slick for it to climb out. It just sat there, looking at him with its head cocked to the side.

E.J. would never have told his parents about the bite but his father walked in while his thumb was still bleeding and his mother went totally postal. It was rabid, she knew it, she never wanted E.J. to have the filthily little thing, yada, yada, yada. She wanted to kill Herman. His father wanted to take him back to the pet store and talk to the owner, find out if E.J. really would need to take rabies shots. When he did, the owner just smiled, said mice often "nip" at their owners, almost as a sign of affection. The beast absolutely did *not* have rabies. *Could not* have rabies. He'd had the mouse for almost a month and the incubation period was ten days to two weeks, so if there'd been anything wrong with it, the disease would have shown by now.

E.J.'s mother demanded the death penalty for Herman anyway, and no amount of pleading, crying and wailing on E.J.'s part could change her mind. He hadn't watched his father kill Herman in the garage, but was looking when he came out holding Herman by the tail and walked out toward the trash cans behind the house.

As soon as his father returned to the house, E.J. sneaked out and found Herman's body, harboring the fantasy that he'd find the mouse alive and be able to nurse it back to health. Herman was lying on top of the latest deposit of plastic bag. He lifted the mouse gently, noted the blood coming from his mouth — refused to notice that his shape wasn't right, meaning his father had stomped … The body was still warm but he wasn't breathing. E.J. stood there holding it as it cooled off, wishing for all the world that there was something he could do to save his little friend. Then he made a little grave for it in the backyard and buried it.

E.J. didn't exactly decide that day to become a vet, but as he got older he never even considered any other profession.

As E.J. sat with his back against the wall of Judd's barn, the agony from his savaged leg literally taking his breath away, his mind flashed to Herman. But only briefly, then the image was gone, replaced by the image of Buster, his head wagging from side to side, foam dripping from his open mouth.

You see, the problem was that Buster wasn't the only one who hadn't gotten his rabies vaccination booster shot. Neither had E.J.

Rabies vaccine was routinely given to people at high risk of exposure to the disease. Veterinarians topped that list. As did other animal handlers, and spelunkers because bats were the primary reservoir of rabies in the animal world. Pre-exposure protection required three doses of rabies vaccine. That's how E.J. knew the shots weren't administered in the stomach. He'd gotten his first in the arm, and when a rash developed around the site, he got the next one in his hip. Changing the location of the shot made no difference. Within an hour after the injection, E.J. got really sick. Maybe even sicker than all the people who'd ridden the Jabberwock to the Middle of Nowhere. Multiple symptoms. Blinding headaches, nausea so severe he was finally dry-heaving blood, so dizzy he couldn't walk.

The agonizing joint pain he experienced gave him a permanent compassion for old people with arthritis, and he spiked a fever of 102 degrees.

His doctor said that clearly E.J. was allergic to some component of the vaccine and would very likely have a severe reaction to the third pre-exposure shot — as if what he'd already experienced wasn't severe enough.

"It could result in Guillain-Barre syndrome," the doctor said and that'd gotten E.J.'s attention. Guillain-Barre left you paralyzed for weeks, months ... sometimes years.

When the doctor recommended that E.J. not take the shot, E.J. was all over that. After all, if he were exposed to the virus, he could then submit to the four-shot regimen of the vaccine and the additional rabies immune globulin (RIG) shot and suffer through whatever reaction it caused. It'd be worth it then, since an allergic reaction — however severe — would still be a small price to pay for not getting rabies! The post-exposure regime of shots had a success rate of 99.9 percent.

The same percentage of people, as a matter of fact, who died if they got rabies.

Chapter Twenty-Two

Judd wanted to do more for E.J., but there didn't seem to be anything more he could do. He wasn't gonna bleed to death and Buster couldn't get at them long's they stayed in here.

But that part about the vaccination. He wanted to ask E.J. more about it, 'cause surely he misunderstood what he'd said, that he hadn't got his own booster. Veterinarians always kept up their shots — E.J. wasn't an idiot. He musta heard him wrong.

"Who knows you're out here, would be like to come looking for you when you don't come back?" he asked.

E.J. looked at him, squinted, and then reached up and felt around, apparently just missing his glasses.

"Nobody. Tried calling. You didn't pick up. Blew out of the office to come see what was the matter with Buster and didn't stop to tell anybody where I was going." He had trouble talking. The pain had to be incredible.

"I guess that's good. Ain't no way to warn them, don't want nobody else walking up here like you done, right into ..."

And then all the air was sucked out of the room. His chest was suddenly so constricted, Judd felt like he was trying to breathe through a straw.

"It ain't ... no, today ain't ... oh, dear God in heaven, it *is*!" He literally cried out the rest. "It's Friday. I's so caught up in what was wrong with Buster, I didn't even think ... Oh, god. Oh dear God."

"Judd, what's wrong?"

"Julie and Michelle. They're ... they might be coming over ..."

"Doreen's girls?"

"Sometimes on Fridays, she brings them by and drops them at the end of the lane to hang out with me while she goes to a cooking class. Eula Mae Reynolds, lives on Cicada Springs Road out by Bennettville, has been teaching her and some of her friends how to make home-made bread and rolls and pie crusts and the like, started right after Christmas."

He couldn't think. His mind was suddenly whirling in such a cyclone of fear he was afraid he was about to vomit, too.

"She lets them girls out at the lane ..." He couldn't finish the sentence because he couldn't finish the thought.

Judd began to pace, back and forth, taking his hat off and wiping his brow and putting it back on and—

E.J. said something Judd didn't hear and he repeated himself.

"*Sometimes?* You said sometimes. Not every Friday."

Judd grabbed hold of the thought like a drowning man going under for the third time.

"No, not every Friday. Depends. Sometimes, Eula Mae has something else to do, but if she don't cancel, Doreen drops the girls off here. It's on the way. Of course, with everything that's been … the Jabberwock and all, ain't nothing for sure."

"How do you know when she …?"

"She always calls first, to tell me they're coming. She'd call."

"And when you don't answer, she won't drop them—"

"No, she'll leave me a message on the machine. She's done that a couple of times. Cause I might be out in the field where I couldn't hear the phone. She knows I'm always home, don't never go nowhere …"

Judd could not keep his thoughts in order. They were skittering around so fast, and the terror he felt grew as the thoughts spun faster and faster.

"Oh dear God, dear God."

"Judd, focus!" He looked at the young man sitting on the floor at his feet and tried to do what he said, but he couldn't grab the thoughts.

"… time will they come?"

Judd looked at his watch and thought his heart might rip out of his chest and drop there on the floor in front of him.

"It's one-fifteen!" Judd didn't even recognize his own voice. "Doreen has to be at Eula Mae's at two and it don't take but about ten minutes to get there from here. So she drops the girls off between one-thirty and a quarter of two."

He had to stop for breath because all that he'd had in his lungs was gone. "That's only … only fifteen minutes from now."

"*If* they're coming, and you don't know that. Judd, listen to me, you don't know that."

Judd stood still, staring down at E.J.

His whole world dropped out from under him, left dangling by a thread over all the burning fires of hell itself.

"The phone rang. After I got stuck in here, before you showed up, the phone rang."

"You don't know it was …"

"I don't know anything except I got to kill that dog!" He *had to* kill Buster. Somehow, some way. "I got to get my rifle and put that dog down."

He actually took a step toward the door before E.J. stopped him.

"Judd, you can't go out there. Buster will kill you if you do."

"I got to get my gun," he repeated. That's what he had to do. He had to go get his gun and—

"Judd, listen to me!" E.J. reached over and grabbed the leg of Judd's pants. "Get down here, look at me."

Judd dropped to his knees beside E.J.

"You have to stay here or Buster will rip you apart like that goose."

"But I got to—"

"You will be *dead!* Buster will kill you, and then when the girls get here, he will kill them—"

"Noooo," Judd screamed, actually screamed. He shook his head, flinging out of it imagined images of two little girls walking up the lane and Buster, standing there, waiting for them, his white fur stained with E.J.'s blood. And Judd's.

"You won't do the girls any good dead."

"But I can't just do *nothing*—"

"Of course not. We'll think of something, but we have to do that, Judd. Are you with me? Are you tracking? We have to think now, plan what to do."

Judd looked into the intense eyes of the young man who sat in the dirt.

"Get hold of yourself, man, we have to make a plan."

"Yes, a plan." Judd said the words before he really

connected any meaning to them. But then he did. E.J. was right. They had only a few minutes to figure out something, to come up with some way to kill Buster before—

"And we're not even sure they're coming," E.J. said. "Hold onto that thought, Judd."

Judd tried, he really did. But somewhere down in the bowels of who he was, his gut, his soul, he knew they were coming. With an absolute certainty that owed nothing at all to reality, Judd knew those two little girls would come walking up that lane in fifteen or twenty minutes. Somehow, he had to kill Buster before they did.

"You have to calm down, Judd. Think. What have we got to fight with?"

"My guns are in the house on the gun rack. I was trying to think what I could use in here, trying to figure."

He looked around the barn. There was almost nothing in it.

There was no pitchfork, though there was a hay loft with bay doors that opened out toward the house.

"I got that." He pointed to a hoe.

There was no machete, but there was a tire iron, could be used as a club. He saw E.J.'s eyes go to the tractor.

"We could get on the tractor and—"

"I done thought of that, thought about driving out the door, or just crashing through the door, try to run over him, or run *from* him, get to the house for my gun. But that dog's quick as lightening. Even wobbly like he is, I couldn't run over him. He's used to dodging away from the tractor's wheels. He'll jump right up on the thing. Ain't no cage, nothing to stop him. He'd be all over me."

"What's attached to the tractor?"

"The PTO shaft's hooked up but ain't nothin' on it."

PTO stood for power take-off, an eight-foot metal rod about six inches in diameter sticking out of the back of the tractor a couple of feet off the ground. It was what attached the tractor to the farm equipment — bush hogs, hay balers, harrows, manure spreaders — that didn't have engines. They got power for their moving parts from the tractor by way of the power take-off shaft. As soon as you cranked the tractor, the PTO shaft would begin to spin, whirling around at the speed of the tractor's engine, something like nine times per second, so fast it was just a blur. Ralph Swanson got his shirt sleeve caught in one and it yanked his arm clean off.

Judd knew E.J. was trying to figure some way to use the tractor to kill the dog, but none of the pieces of equipment that had blades or knives — tillers, discs, cultivators — were hooked up. And even if they hadn't been sitting in the shed beside the barn, no way was Buster stupid enough to just stand there and let you run over him.

The tractor'd be no use. They'd have to find some other way to kill him.

Chapter Twenty-Three

"How are we moving?" Charlie's voice sounded very small.

Nobody answered. They didn't have to.

The mist. Even without reference points outside the windows, it was clear the car was moving forward. They all felt it. Charlie had her foot on the brake, pushed all the way to the floor as if somehow she could stop the car's forward motion.

The car kept moving, farther and farther from the spot where Charlie'd stopped to avoid driving through the mist. It seemed to Charlie that the car was moving forward faster than it had been at first. How did you judge speed when you could see nothing? But it *seemed* ... no it *was*, the car was moving faster and faster, gaining speed with every second.

The shapes were still whirling around and around the car in the milky white, impossibly dark and sparkling at the same time, but the wailing and whispering had grown faint as soon as they heard the thump.

The tone of the faint wails and whispers had changed from angry back to sad and forlorn. Charlie tried following just one of the shapes with her eyes, studying just one instead of all of them, hoping to make out some kind of detail. But now they were floating around the car too fast for that. Spinning around and around as the car hurled forward faster and faster.

The car stopped — so abruptly, they all lurched forward, testimony to how fast the car'd been traveling.

Even before they settled back into their seats, there was another thump. It was sudden and loud and very real-world. No shapes-in-the-mist, ethereal quality to it. It came from the area of the trunk of the car and with the sound, Charlie felt the back of the car begin to lift up, while the front end began to point downward.

Her heart had been hammering a hole in her chest and now the beats blended into a single loud hum of horror. Terror grabbed hold of her belly and squeezed so tight she couldn't get her breath. She shot Malachi a terrified look but it was so dark in the car she couldn't see … Dark and cold. *Cold!* Yes, it was cold here, too. The back of the car rose higher. Her breath frosted when she gasped and she couldn't hold onto the scream any longer.

"Stoooop it!"

The movement stopped. The dark shapes stopped spinning and faded back into the milky white. The car hung there with the back end high in the air. One second. Two. Then the front end began to lift, the back went downward, and the shocks engaged when the weight of the car again settled on them.

"What the—?" Harry began, but Malachi put his fingers to his lips and whispered harshly, "Shhhhh."

Charlie strained to hear, but the whispers, the cries — all the sound had stopped.

The milk white outside the windows turned gray. It swirled, like wind rippling through wheat. The light grew.

Charlie could make out Malachi's face now and outside the car there were shapes ... trees. The mist was thinning.

And then it was gone, like turning a blow dryer on the condensation on a bathroom mirror.

They could see out the car windows.

Charlie's throat seized up or she would have shrieked this time.

There was no road in front of the car, just empty air.

She rolled down her window and stuck her head out. Beyond the car lay a jagged rip in the road. The front tire was an inch from the end of the pavement.

"Everybody get out of the car slowly," Malachi said.

They eased open the doors and stepped out onto firm asphalt, then walked gingerly forward and looked off the edge of the "rip." A hunk of asphalt twenty feet wide was missing from the road, had been torn away when the land beneath it collapsed, eaten away by the raging water of a flooded creek.

The front tires of the car rested just about as close as it was possible to get to the jagged edge of the asphalt.

"Anybody wanna tell me what just happened?" Roscoe asked. Charlie was sure his voice was less firm than he would have liked.

"It's pretty clear *what* happened," Malachi said.

His voice was level. He didn't appear to be in the least rattled or troubled by what had just happened. She supposed it was the military training. Though he came home saddled with raging PTSD episodes that took him out of reality and dropped him back into a nightmare of his own making or his own remembrance, he was clearly here and present now. And also clearly not as shaken as the others were.

"The issue isn't what, but how. Why, maybe, too. And

all of those questions are getting worn very thin in my mind because I've been using them a lot lately."

"Something picked up the car with us in it and very nearly—" Harry began.

"Would it have?" Roscoe wondered aloud. "Would it have dumped us over the edge or was it just trying to scare us?"

That was what you heard, in tales about the haints in Fearsome Hollow. That they were … not *pranksters*, that was too gentle and benign a word, but the stories did have a through-line of mischief that appeared to be just for effect.

"It was gonna do it," Harry said. "It was gonna dump us in the creek until Charlie here rebuked it."

Rebuke wasn't a word you heard every day.

"You think that because I—?"

"Yes, ma'am, I absolutely do think it stopped because you told it to. Scolded it."

"But why—?"

"Ahhhh, now see, there's that threadbare word again," Malachi said.

"I don't think it was the mist," she said. "I think it was something *in* the mist, something hidden by the mist. Something … other."

That was a conversation stopper. No one else spoke.

Malachi got behind the wheel and piloted the car around the broken piece of asphalt, wouldn't let anybody get back in until he was fifty feet beyond the cut. Then he returned the car to Charlie and as she prepared to put it in gear, Roscoe said they ought to take Frogtown Road out to Route 19, down it to Sword's Creek Road that'd lead them back to Byrne Lane. Charlie didn't know what difference it made, as long as they left Fearsome Hollow—

"You're in *my* patch. Get out!"

She jerked around, looking to see who had spoken. "Did you hear that?"

Malachi was in the front on the passenger side, fishing around for his seatbelt in the cracks of the cushion and he had frozen at the words.

"Hear what?" Roscoe asked.

"I didn't hear nothing," said Harry.

"The wind," Malachi said, fastening his belt. "Buckle up." He looked at Charlie when he spoke again. "Let's get out of this *patch* and back to the rest of the world."

THE AGONY IN E.J.'s leg made it hard to concentrate on anything else. Until Judd told him about his granddaughters. The pain seemed to dial down after that.

He knew the little girls. E.J.'d performed complicated bowel surgery on Doreen's cocker spaniel, Benji, and for a couple of months, she'd brought the girls with her when she brought the dog in for weekly follow-up appointments. The girls reminded E.J. of the children he had seen in Scotland. During his brief marriage, he and his soon-to-be not-wife had traveled there to see the Highlands.

It was a stereotype that Scottish children had rosy cheeks. But stereotypes were stereotypes for a reason, and it seemed that everywhere he looked there were little girls with bright blue eyes, pigtails, braids and cheeks so red you'd swear they were chapped and in desperate need of lotion. Lovely, delicate children. They'd made him want children of his own. They'd touched his heart.

Julie and Michelle Shepperson were like that. Whenever he saw Benji on the appointment list he smiled, looked forward to the little girls' inquisitiveness, had shown them and explained the function of every piece of equipment in the exam room.

Julie had delicate features and big brown eyes. Michelle had pixie features, too, with a little turned-up nose and blue eyes… and yes, both of the children had rosy cheeks. He was certain that by now, Julie was bemoaning that fact. Teetering on the brink of teenager-dom as she was, she would likely spend the next decade hiding the roses under a layer of makeup. But maybe rosy cheeks went the way of baby fat during adolescence. He didn't know, but did know that when he ran into Doreen and the girls coming out of Foodtown right after Christmas, Julie had had earphones in her ears and her brand new iPod dangling around her neck, singing along with some song he wouldn't likely recognize if he heard it and the lyrics of which were unquestionably inappropriate for a not-yet thirteen-year-old child.

Julie and Michelle.

The brief image he had gotten of Buster … He had glanced back when the dog bit into his leg, cast a look over his shoulder that couldn't have lasted a second but that burned an image into his brain as permanent as a brand on a cow.

The dog's eyes were glazed. Its white fur was splotched with blood. The goose's and whatever other animals it had killed. And E.J.'s blood. He saw his own blood squirt out onto the dog's snout, a frozen second that lasted a lifetime, as the rabid beast sunk his teeth into E.J.'s leg. The *mad dog*.

E.J. IS FASCINATED by Wanda Jablonski's curls. She is seated two rows ahead of him and one row over, right in the shaft of sunlight shining into the freshman lab class, the one right after lunch that he only manages not to sleep through by concentrating on Wanda's hair.

Wanda is no beauty queen, but she does have the most beautiful hair he has ever seen. A pale blonde, the color of Marilyn Monroe's hair, a blonde so pale there is almost no color at all. It hangs down to the middle of her back in long ringlets that—

"… you hear the question, Mr. Hamilton?"

He was zoning, and Dr. Hildenbrand had caught him.

"Yes sir. I mean, no sir, I didn't hear—"

"I was instructing the class what to do if they chanced to wake up some morning and see a bat on their ceiling."

"A bat on the ceiling, sir?"

"A bat. Yes. Ugly little creatures that fly around eating insects and not running into walls because they have sonar. What should you do, Mr. Hamilton, in that circumstance?"

"I guess … get a broom maybe and sweep it off—"

"Wrong! What you should do, Mr. Hamilton, is haul your worthless butt to the nearest emergency room and get them to administer the rabies anti-venom. Bats have little tiny teeth, surely you've noticed." *The professor had never particularly liked E.J. and E.J.'s inattention had just put a gigantic "kick me" sign on his own back and handed Dr. Hildenbrand a cowboy boot.*

"Yes sir, I have seen how small a bat's—"

"That bat on your ceiling could have bitten you in the night, and because the puncture wounds would be so small, you might not even have noticed them."

"I suppose that's true, sir."

"And given the likelihood that any given bat you happen to run across in the wild is likely to be rabid, it would behoove you to take the prudent precautions, is that not true?"

"Yes sir." *E.J. does not tell him about his allergic reaction to the first of the two shots he'd been given.*

"Why don't you describe for the benefit of your fellow students, exactly what will happen to you if you fail to take the necessary, prudent precautions. If you blow it off, go on about your day, go to the* *game that night, get drunk afterwards and"* — he glances at Wanda Jablonski — *"indulge your hormone-driven proclivities."*

"The first dose of the vaccine should be administered within the first twenty-four hours after exposure," E.J. says.

"But what if you feel fine?"

"The incubation period can be a few days ... or a few months."

"Incubation period?"

The professor is making fun of him. He can sense his fellow students withdrawing from the confrontation. They don't want to be caught in a crossfire so they all became potted plants.

"The time between when you are exposed to the virus and when you show symptoms of the disease."

"And what happens after you show symptoms?"

"... you ... die. It's almost a hundred percent fatal."

"And between those first symptoms and when you succumb, what will happen to you?"

E.J. wracks his brain, has to get the symptoms right and in the right order.

"First, there will be a tingling, prickling or itching feeling around the bite area. Then ... maybe flu-like symptoms. A fever, headache, muscle aches, nausea, tiredness."

"And after that?"

"Anxiety. Confusion. Agitation. Hallucinations. Paralysis. In most cases a ... fear of water—"

"Hence the name, hydrophobia."

"Which is followed two to ten days after the onset of symptoms by delirium, coma and death."

"Ah, yes. A coma. Not terribly unlike your natural state, is it, Mr. Hamilton?"

BOTTOM LINE REALITY CHECK HERE: E.J. had taken only two of the required three rabies shots. And that had been more than a decade ago. He had never taken a booster. He had no vaccination-conferred immunity to the disease, had always balanced the risk he was taking with the risk of a massive allergic reaction.

And in a normal world, where the universe functioned in a predictable fashion, that would not be a death sentence. Yes, he was allergic to the vaccine and forced to take not only the whole four-shot regime given to people who'd not been vaccinated, but an additional shot called RIG, rabies immune globulin, he would be one sick puppy. Would need to check into the hospital because he was sure an allergic reaction of that magnitude would put him into anaphylactic shock.

But an allergic reaction was treatable. Anaphylactic shock was treatable. A shot of epinephrine and he had a greater than ninety-five percent chance of survival.

Buster's bite was not treatable.

It was not survivable.

Without the intervention of the vaccine — the first dose of it administered in the next twenty-four hours … *riiight* — E.J. would die of rabies.

But he had longer to live than the two little girls who any minute now might come waltzing up the lane … into the jaws of a monstrous beast that would tear them apart as surely as it had dismembered that goose.

Chapter Twenty-Four

Fish had to do it. He had to do it now and he had to do it right. He couldn't screw this up.

He had staggered away from Martha Whittiker's house back to the basement of the Methodist church, and was clutching the bottle of whiskey he'd stolen, planning to get as blind drunk as it was possible to get, given that he was so alcohol-saturated drunkenness often totally eluded him.

He'd unscrewed the lid before it hit him.

The process of getting back across the Ridge to the basement of the Methodist church undetected, and it was hot outside, had resulted in and necessitated some small bit of sobering up. He had managed to make it behind fences and bushes, no stagger-walking down open sidewalks, in large part because he was like the potted plant that sat beside the door that you never noticed until your lack of attention had turned it into a black stump. Folks just didn't notice Fish.

But folks would notice Martha Whittiker. She had such a squeaky little voice it was almost cartoonish, was so sweet sugar wouldn't melt in her mouth, patting people on the arm and saying, "Bless your heart!" When she started sharing her tale of woe about how Fish had knocked her unconscious and stolen her booze, there would be an outcry of some sort.

The severity of it would depend on the degree to which she had been injured and how penitent Fish became.

His whole way of life was dependent on the goodwill of other people. They provided shelter, a meager amount of sustenance, afforded him the life he had chosen.

If he were seen as *dangerous* …

And what if she … what? Pressed charges for assault? With whom? As he had already worked out in his head, the lack of a functioning judiciary, coupled with all-but-nonexistent law enforcement, would make punishment for any crime unlikely. Impossible, really.

But folks being wary of him was sufficient punishment, would destroy his whole world.

He had to go back, had to throw himself on her mercy, and ask her to forgive him.

And he would have to … gulp … *return* what he had stolen from her. That was the hardest part of all, of course. He didn't mind humbling himself before grandmotherly Martha Whittiker, but the Maker's Mark! He would never see the like again. Not an exaggeration. It might be the only bottle in the whole county and giving it up was a sacrifice he'd make only for self-preservation.

He went to her front door, just walked down the sidewalk to her door and lifted his hand to knock and promptly chickened out. Or was drowning from the mouthwatering nearness of the bottle of Maker's he carried and had been rendered temporarily unable to speak.

He turned, went back down the porch steps and forced himself to go down the driveway to the kitchen door, pausing only to peek in the garage apartment window to be sure her grandson hadn't come around. He hadn't even moved.

Fish wouldn't have to knock on the back door. He'd left it unlocked. He could just crack it open an inch or two and call out her name, shout his apology before she ever looked on his face.

Yes, that was a better plan.

He stood on the stoop in front of the kitchen door, turned the handle and opened the door only about two inches.

"Mrs. Whittiker. It's me, Fish, and I have come to beg your forgiveness for the terrible way I treated you when last I was here."

He expected to hear the pat, pat, pat of her rapid foot-steps into the kitchen to fling the door open and start yelling at him.

He heard nothing but silence.

"Mrs. Whittiker?"

Nothing.

He pushed the door inward enough to peer around it.

"Mrs. Whiiiiitiker?"

Then he stepped into the kitchen, and when he did he saw Mrs. Whittiker. She was lying right where he'd left her. The puddle of blood spread out around her was consider-ably bigger than it'd been then, but she hadn't moved.

She was still unconscious.

No, she wasn't. She wasn't unconscious. She was …

He had *killed* her. He literally staggered backward at the sight of her body, dropped to his knees and let the grocery sack slip out of his numb fingers, overcome by remorse and sorrow. No! Noooo! He couldn't … he *wouldn't* … but he had. Oh dear holy God he had not just hurt this woman, he had taken her life.

Poor Martha Whittiker would never see another

sunrise, would never laugh that squeaky little laugh, wouldn't bake cookies or knit sweaters or … He had stolen all her tomorrows.

He didn't realize he was sobbing until he felt the tears wet on his cheeks, and then he gave in to them, put his head in his hands and bawled like a baby.

He had *killed* her.

Just like he had killed—

No! He slammed that door shut so hard the bang must surely have been an audible sound in the room. The door was buried deep in the darkest pit of Holmes Fischer's being, hidden in forever-night, and he was no longer aware of the bright kitchen as he planted his back against the nightmare door, braced his feet, held it closed with every bit of strength he possessed. What lay on the other side of that door was madness. To see it, to know it, to remember it was to shatter his mind, his psyche … his soul. He drank to forget what was behind that door, to blur the memories, erase the pain and the terror.

He wasn't aware of reaching into the grocery sack on the floor beside him and grabbing the bottle of Maker's Mark. Ripping off the lid, he turned it up and gulped it down so fast he choked and strangled and the amber liquid dripped off his chin.

The swallowing motion calmed, the burning liquid soothed. The familiar fuzzy warmth began to return. The door in the dark no longer strained at the hinges and Fish was able to crawl slowly back up out of that place into the light.

And in the light lay the body of poor little Martha Whittiker.

He hadn't intended to *hurt* her! He was supposed to be long gone before she even got home. It had been an *accident,* not his fault.

But she was dead!

And if you killed somebody when they caught you stealing from them …

Suddenly he couldn't breathe.

If finding out he'd stolen from Mrs. Whittiker would make folks wary of him, what if they knew he'd *killed* her?

What could he *do?* Would anybody understand that he had meant no harm? Would anybody believe it had been an accident? Particularly when he was blurry on the details of exactly what *did* happen.

What could he—?

That's when the brilliant idea struck him. In his usual sodden state, the brilliant ideas almost never made it all the way to the higher centers of his brain for him to consider them. He wasn't sober now, but he was certainly not as inebriated as he would have liked and this one made it through.

Just an image. A face, but it was enough. Dylan Shaw.

The kid was stoned. So stoned that if his grandmother's body suddenly *appeared* in his living room, he'd have no idea how it got there. You could march the U.S. Marine Drum and Bugle Corps through the apartment right now and he wouldn't notice.

Most important, he was *just a kid* — what, seventeen maybe? More likely sixteen. Lynch mobs didn't hang children. He was certain the code of human chivalry would frown on such behavior.

Liam Montgomery was the county's only duly sworn law enforcement officer and it took that poor boy an hour and a half to watch *60 Minutes.* Would he/could he even arrest the boy? Not likely. Fish wouldn't be consigning a drugged-out teenager to a lifetime behind bars for a crime he didn't commit. Even Fish had not sunk low enough to do a thing like *that.* At least not yet. But he didn't mind at all getting the boy blamed for his grandmother's death to ensure that nobody went looking for the person who really *did* kill her. Where was the harm in that if the boy would suffer no consequences for the crime? The county was without a legal system right now, and by the time it had one again, if it ever did, it'd be too late to gather enough evidence to make a case. The boy would get off.

And nobody would ever know Holmes Fischer was even in the neighborhood.

For the world to be convinced Mrs. Whittiker met her untimely death in her grandson's apartment out back, there could be no evidence to the contrary here in her kitchen.

Fish would have to clean up the mess. And wipe his fingerprints off … Nobody in Nowhere County had a fingerprint kit.

Clean up the mess, and get rid of the body.

He screwed the lid back on the bottle of Maker's and set it back in the grocery sack. He wouldn't have to give it up. That alone was payment in full for what he was going to have to do next — which was sober up enough not to screw up, clean up after a … a murder.

And get rid of the body.

Chapter Twenty-Five

Judd was talking and E.J. had to tune out the agony of his leg and the screaming in his head to listen.

"… see them from there."

"See the girls?"

"Up in the loft. Open that door and you can see down the hill to the bottom of the lane."

"So you could climb up there, yell at Doreen, tell her—"

"She couldn't hear me yell, not from here." He looked like a horrible thought had just occurred to him. And it had. "Julie's got that thing, that iWhatever thing stuck in her ears all the time, listening to music. She wouldn't hear me yelling if I was standing five feet away!"

E.J. remembered the iPod.

"We got to kill Buster, now, right now. I keep the guns on my gun rack loaded. I get in the house, I could grab my deer rifle in ten seconds."

A shot from a deer rifle would drop the dog in its tracks.

"I gotta get me that gun."

That was it, then, there wasn't any way around it.

"Is there any other door out of the barn?"

"Just the big'uns." Two bay doors swung opened on the front of the barn, big enough to admit the tractor, farm equipment, and the occasional cow or sheep. Those doors were fastened shut now with a hasp on the inside.

"That it? Just those?" E.J. gestured toward the bay doors.

"You could jump outta the hay loft."

"So the only way in or out—?"

"There's a hole in the wall, over there behind that barrel. I hit it with the edge of the tobacco setter and knocked some boards loose and Buster liked to dug his way in here through it."

"Could you get out that way?"

"Me? Crawl through that hole?"

"If you had to, could you do it?

"Yeah, I guess. I could kick out another board or two … if I had to. Why?"

"Because I have a plan — not a very good one, but it's the only shot we have."

It didn't take E.J. long to explain what he had in mind and he watched Judd's eyes grow bigger and bigger as he spoke.

"A skinny guy like me, I'll fit," E.J. said.

"What makes you think you can outrun—?"

"I don't, actually. That last part is just … you know, a Hail Mary. I figure he'll take me down as soon as I turn around and start running … well, hobbling."

"But E.J., if Buster gets you, he'll kill—"

"He's already killed me, Judd. It'll take a while, but I'm as good as dead."

"What are you talk—?"

"Rabies. I told you — I'm not vaccinated."

"You're what! A veterinarian and you—?"

"A long story, Judd, and we don't have time for me to tell it."

"But … but even if you ain't had the vaccination … folks get bit all the time who ain't been vaccinated and they give 'em—"

"Medication that, to my knowledge, is not available anywhere in Nowhere County."

"You ain't got any at—?"

"I'm a vet, Judd. I treat animals, not people. You don't go to a vet if you get bitten by a dog, you go to the emergency room. The rabies immune globulin is available in hospitals. Oh, the hospital in Carlisle might not have any on hand, I suppose, but they could send off to Lexington to get it if they don't."

"And you can't go …?" It was beginning to settle in on Judd, but he still fought it. "The Jabberwock ain't always gonna be there. Soon's it—"

"We could debate this all day. It's my opinion that Nowhere County is stuck with the Jabberwock—"

"For good?"

"Just my opinion, but it doesn't have to stay here forever to cook my goose, as the phrase goes. The incubation period for rabies in a human is a week, maybe two weeks — depending on the amount of the virus … and Buster gave me a big dose. First shot needs to be administered within the first twenty-four hours. Once you start showing symptoms … it's over. There's not a thing they can do for you. Best doctors in the best hospital in the world would just have to stand by your bed and watch you die."

Judd just looked at him, flabbergasted.

"It's an ugly way to die, Judd."

"So's getting your throat ripped out by a dog," Judd whispered.

"True that. I'd rather die in my sleep at some time after my one-hundredth birthday. As soon as Buster took a hunk out of my leg, that stopped being an option. Of the available options, I pick number two. It's the only chance we have to save Julie and Michelle."

Judd actually backed up a step, shaking his head.

"I don't know about this, E.J. ..."

"Yes, you do, Judd. You do. You don't like it and neither do I. But you know. If you've got a better plan, let's hear it. If you don't, you need to start that tractor and engage the power take-off, unfasten the clasp on the bay doors and then haul your butt up into that loft to watch for the girls."

He paused.

"They might not even come today, you know that, in which case the best laid plans of mice and men ..."

"Huh?"

"Never mind. Just get up into that loft." E.J. looked at his watch and couldn't see the numbers on it. He'd lost his glasses ... somewhere. "How much time do we have?"

Judd looked at his own watch and all the color washed out of his face.

"Maybe ten minutes."

E.J. extended his hand to Judd. "Then help me up and get after it."

Judd pulled E.J. to his feet, with all his weight on his right leg. The room swam in and out of focus as soon as he was upright, a loud *whahm, whahm, whahm* sound echoed in his head and he was almost overcome by a wave of nausea. He reached out his other hand to the door behind him to steady himself.

"Shoot, you can't even stand up. How you think you're gonna outrun—"

"My problem, Judd. Go!"

They stood for a moment, eyes locked. E.J. saw tears well up in Judd's. He still had E.J.'s hand in his and he grasped it with the other hand, too, stood holding it in both of his. E.J. felt the calluses on Judd's hands, a farmer's hands. Judd shook his hand slowly, paused, then let go, resolutely turned and ran toward the tractor.

Chapter Twenty-Six

She was dead.

She was. Grandma Whittiker wasn't breathing, which meant she was dead. But you could start somebody back breathing if you knew how and he didn't know how, but if you did you could start their hearts and get them to breathe again with that thing — CPR, that thing — but he didn't take the class the fire department offered because he was somewhere else, he didn't remember where else, but somewhere, so he didn't learn how to do the thing, the CPR thing.

If not-breathing was why they was dead, you could bring them back.

But Dylan didn't think her not breathing was why his grandmother was dead. It was the other way around. She was dead and that was why she wasn't breathing. She was dead, she was, you could tell, just look at her, and she felt cold, which meant even if he'd known how to get somebody to start breathing again after they'd stopped it wouldn't do no good because she was already dead.

Stop it.

Stop it!

Dylan literally grabbed hold of his hair at his temples and pulled, like that would stop the thoughts that were racing around inside his skull so fast he couldn't think them, didn't have time to think them, was afraid maybe them spinning around and around in there so fast like that could cause enough friction to set his hair on fire. That was crazy.

It was the meth, that was why he couldn't think. No, he could think. That was the problem, he could think but there were too many thoughts and he had to stop them, slow them down because he had to think them. Had to figure out what to do.

Grandma was dead. She was dead, her body cold, had been that way when he woke up and found her on the floor, and he didn't know what she'd died of.

Except he did, sort of. He'd been snorting and shooting up, getting all kinda high after he stole that stash of Buddy's and brought it home to party down. That had been yesterday. No, the day before. No yesterday, and he'd been *flying* … oooooh doggies, he'd been up there and then …

Then *what?*

Dylan didn't know.

He couldn't remember.

Think, he had to think. He had to remember.

He'd got high and then …

There was nothing there. Blank. He didn't know what'd happed between when he got high and him waking up here on the floor beside his grandmother and her body was cold and she wasn't breathing and he didn't know how to start her breathing again but even if he did it didn't matter because she was dead.

Dead!

Mad Dog

Dead with blood. Blood everywhere. Her blood or his or maybe somebody else's altogether but there was blood and her hair was all matted with it so she didn't just die in her sleep, have a heart attack or a stroke or whatever it was that old people did who went to sleep and didn't wake up. That wasn't it. She had died of something violent and Dylan couldn't remember what it was.

But somebody'd killed her. Killed her. Murdered her.

Somebody.

Who? And if they killed her, maybe they were still here, waiting, lurking somewhere in the shadows, waiting …

Dylan dropped to the floor and put his arms over his head to shield it and screamed, "Please don't, no, don't!"

But there was no sound after that except his own ragged breathing and he looked up and there was nobody standing there with the axe about to chop into him with it. Or a knife about to stab him. Or a gun about to shoot him. Wasn't nobody there at all. Except his sweet little old grandmother. And she was dead.

She was dead and her white hair wasn't white anymore but red and not from red hair dye. It was red from the blood that'd come out of a — *head wound!* — after somebody hit her or hacked her or stabbed her or something!

He had rolled away from her as soon as he realized she was cold because she was dead and now he was huddled in the corner of the filthy room, looking at her body on the floor and knowing that the blood was hers and that's why she was dead.

Somebody was screaming, wailing. Crying out in terror.

And he realized it was him. He was the one screaming, huddled there in the corner of the filthy room with Grandma's bloody dead body on the floor, and what was Dylan going to do?

He clamped his hands over his mouth to stop himself from screaming. Shook his head as if to clear it, but that was like shaking the pieces of a puzzle in a can and thinking that'd fit them all together again. It only made the random firing thoughts fire faster.

Dead. She's dead.

And …

And …

Then his thoughts slowed. He'd ridden a carnival ride once with a rollercoaster that went faster and faster until you were screaming even though you didn't mean to but the scream was ripped out of your throat and then at the bottom the rollercoaster car hit water—

The car hit water and slowed down.

Hit the water, splashed water everywhere and slowed down.

His thoughts slowed down like that now. Felt like some of them slammed into the backs of others of them, the ones behind that were still going fast hitting the ones in the front that had hit the water and slowed down.

Grandma was dead.

She was dead because somebody had killed her.

He thought that last thought so slow it seemed to take a hundred years to think it.

Somebody had killed Grandma.

Somebody had … what? Didn't shoot her, he didn't think. He couldn't see the wound on her head but he'd bet it wasn't round like a bullet made the hole. What then? An axe? A machete? A meat cleaver? Hacked Grandma in the head with an axe and got pieces of her skull and hair and brain on the axe and that had killed her.

Who killed Grandma?

Who hit Grandma with the bloody axe?

Then the slow thoughts stopped altogether. He sat

cowering in the corner of the room not thinking anything at all. Maybe you had to be thinking something to think you weren't thinking anything but his mind appeared to be totally empty. Hollow.

It was empty, like the gym at school after they turned off the lights and you walked across the floor in the dark and your steps echoed off the bleachers.

Like that. Empty. Echoing.

Dylan did not remember killing his grandmother. He didn't remember hitting her in the head with an axe. Or a machete. Or a meat cleaver? But *somebody* did.

Someone had been here with him and Grandma. Someone who hit Grandma with … something, had killed her.

Or he imagined somebody else was here and it had really been him who killed her.

Dylan could almost feel an axe in his hands, a meat cleaver, slippery because it had blood on it.

And then he was running. Across the room, out the door, down the gravel road to the old pickup truck Grandma'd got him — Grandma Whittiker, who was *dead*. He leapt behind the wheel and only then thought to wonder if there were keys in it. But there were keys.

He started the truck, slammed it into gear, pulled out of his grandmother's driveway and went flying down the street, no destination in mind. Driving too fast to keep the truck between the curbs, bounced up into somebody's yard and hit a mailbox, bounced down into the street again and kept going. Then he was out of town and he didn't know how he'd made it down the streets but he was on the highway now and the world passed by the windows in a green smear.

He wasn't going anywhere. Just going.

He had to get away. Just *away*. Anywhere away. He'd go

to Lexington or Cincinnati. Get a bus to … somewhere. Anywhere. He had a debit card in his wallet … if he had his wallet. He had enough money for a ticket to—

The world suddenly turned black, shiny, sparkling black, and his head filled with buzzing static.

Chapter Twenty-Seven

E.J. heard the rumble when Judd cranked the old John Deere tractor to life, heard the *squee* sound and then just the whirring of the spinning shaft when he engaged the power take-off. Judd's was a small barn and he had arranged its limited space to maximum storage. The tractor was jammed up against the far wall, not five inches of clearance between the big wheel and the wall. On the other side was a stack of hay bales six feet high so that Judd had to maneuver the tractor just right so it would fit.

Judd climbed down out of the driver's seat and ran to the bay doors on the front of the barn. He unhooked the hasp. Buster could get into the barn now with the hasp unlocked. If he lunged at the door with the force he'd thrown himself into the side door, the bay would fly instantly inward.

Judd never looked at E.J., just crossed the barn to the ladder leading to the hay loft and climbed it. The interior of the barn suddenly got brighter when E.J. opened the two bay doors on the loft and sunlight streamed in through them.

E.J. wished he had asked Judd to give him something to lean on for a cane or a crutch, but he hadn't thought of it at the time. Without it, the only way he could move forward was hopping on his right leg, the jarring motion sending such agony up from his injured leg he almost couldn't catch his breath.

Gratefully, as he made his way along the wall to the door, he came upon the hoe Judd had used to scoop up E.J.'s vomit, the one he'd pointed out as a useless weapon. Weapon, no; crutch, absolutely. It was just what he needed, with a wide blade on the bottom to grant it stability. E.J. grasped it like a wizard clutching his staff and used it to pull himself along. He would have to move as fast as it was possible to move. The timing on this plan, such as it was, required that he and Judd be in position when they set it in motion.

As soon as Judd spotted Doreen's car letting the girls out at the road — please, dear God, *no*, let one of them be sick or the car break down or an avalanche block the road — he was to call out to E.J., then climb down out of the loft and run to where he had rolled the barrel into place to keep Buster from crashing through the hole in the boards. Once Judd was crouched behind the barrel, ready to roll it out of the way, E.J. would push open the bay doors and … yeah, what? How would he get the attention of the dog? He didn't even know where the animal was, an unasked question that Judd quickly answered.

"Buster's standing next to the oak by the compost heap. Just standing there, shaking his head."

Good. That was actually the best possible position for the dog to be for the plan to work. E.J. would push the two big barn doors open — which would instantly draw the dog's attention. And then yell, jump up and down — okay, not that — but yell until Buster came running. When E.J. turned to run from Buster, Judd would roll the barrel out of the way and crawl out of the barn though the hole. And while E.J. had the dog … *occupied*, Judd would run to the house for his deer rifle, return and shoot the dog dead.

The keeping the dog occupied part. That was … oh, come on … what it meant was that E.J. had to put up enough of a fight as the dog mauled him to keep the dog interested in the kill. And there was, after all, the Hail Mary.

Buster wouldn't be able to see Judd crawl out of the hole, and it was inconceivable that inside the barn … dealing with E.J., he would happen to look up and see Judd hauling butt from the side of the barn to the house. And even if he did, with that kind of head start it was possible Judd could beat the dog there.

If that happened. If he killed E.J. instantly, turned and saw Judd and went after him … well, E.J. hoped the back door on Judd's house was strong enough to stop the charging dog. He'd been inside Judd's kitchen years ago … he had just gotten back to Nowhere County and opened his office, and Judd's old coon dog, Molly, had had a litter of puppies under his kitchen table. But Molly refused to nurse them, wouldn't have anything to do with them, so E.J. had come out to have a look.

He remembered the kitchen smelled of chocolate chip cookies, which Judd's late wife Mildred had made just because she knew he was coming. E.J.'d made the dog a bed out of a cardboard box, a cozy, den-like enclosure, and snuggled it into a far corner of the kitchen, and when he put Molly's puppies in it, the dog hopped in and settled right down to nurse.

E.J. tried now to recall the construction of the door, but

drew a total blank. Hard to remember an ordinary-looking thing like a door and recall how it was constructed years later. It would just have to hold for a few seconds. The den was right next to the kitchen and the gun rack was on the wall in there. All Judd had to do was—

"They're here!" Judd cried from his perch in the hay loft, his voice a high-pitched wail of fear and denial. "Oh, dear God, they're here. She just let them out and they've started up the lane."

Judd crossed the hay loft in like two strides, practically leapt to the barn floor and ran to his position behind the barrel in front of the hole in the wall.

And E.J. reached out and began to push open the barn door.

JULIE WAS LIKE ZERO FUN. Zeee-ro!

All she wanted to do was listen to her stupid music on that stupid iPod. Michelle might as well be by herself because half the time Julie couldn't even hear her. And when she got in Julie's face and made hand motions, got her attention, Julie would yank the earbuds out of her ears in irritation and cry:

"What? Can't you see I'm listening to Bonnie Tyler?"

Michelle had never heard of Bonnie Tyler, didn't care she was singing. All she wanted was for her sister to pay attention to her when she talked. Was that too much to ask? As a matter of fact, it was.

As they started up the lane to Pawpaw's house, Julie was even singing along with the band, the words.

"... *once upon a time I was falling in love, now I'm only falling apart* ..."

Did she have any idea how stupid she sounded, like she

did that time she had strep throat, her voice all hoarse and gravelly. Julie could barely carry a tune anyway and she was off key. Michelle was taking piano lessons and she knew about things like that.

Had been taking piano lessons. Now she sat home and did nothing because that stupid Jabberwock thing kept her mother from taking her to her lessons in Carlisle. Or soccer practice.

Michelle was afraid of the Jabberwock thing, but she didn't tell anybody because she didn't want to sound like a baby. But she had heard the older, bigger kids talking about zombies and the end of the world and aliens and nobody knew what the Jabberwock thing was or when it would go away.

She dreamed about it at night. It was a big, black hairy thing, like a giant hairy worm wrapped all the way around the county, and if you bothered it, it would open its huge mouth, and its breath smelled like rotten eggs, and eat you up and then vomit you back up in the Middle of Nowhere. She'd heard her mother and Mrs. Kramer talking about that, the vomiting part.

And she wanted to talk to Julie about it. Julie always let Michelle get in bed with her when she had a bad dream. And she even once changed the sheets on her bed when Michelle accidentally wet the bed and was so embarrassed, didn't want her mother to know so Jules had put clean sheets on the bed and put the wet ones in the bottom of the laundry basket where her mother wouldn't notice them.

But how could she talk about the Jabberwock, or anything else with Julie if all she did was listen to that stupid music with those things in her ears that made her deaf?

"... total eclipse of the heart ..."

"Well, fine. Be that way. I'm gonna go play with Buster," Michelle said, turned and ran up the lane toward the house, crying, "Buuusss-ter. Here, Buster! C'mere, boy."

Chapter Twenty-Eight

E.J. hadn't had a whole lot of time to consider his decision. As soon as he found out about Michelle and Julie, all the time was gone. They had to do something and this was all E.J. could think to do.

He was going to die anyway. Almost certainly. He'd made it sound more concrete than it really was to Judd because the man might not have gone for the deal if he'd thought E.J. had a chance. And he didn't have much of one. But there was a tiny ray of hope, an itty bitty beam of sun shining down through the black clouds.

All dosages of all medications were based on averages and extrapolations. The common wisdom was that it required three shots of the rabies vaccine to confer immunity. But who was to say that two wouldn't be enough in some cases, his case specifically? Who knew? It wasn't likely, but there was a slender chance.

So he wasn't, in reality, trading one certain death for another. He was trading a little bit of life, a hope and a prayer, for being ripped apart by a mad dog. He'd seen a

Hill Street Blues episode once where this drug dealer who'd rather die than go to prison had acted like he was pulling a gun so the police would have to open fire. He hadn't really had a gun, though, and they said he had committed suicide by cop. E.J. supposed it was fitting that a veterinarian chose suicide by dog.

His mind was spinning around so fast, so many thoughts whizzing by he just sat back and marveled at the parade, didn't make any effort to grab one and think it. He was entertained by the pageantry of the show. That was enough.

Judd cried out then, "They're here!" He could see them, two sweet little girls walking innocently up a lane into the jaws of a monster. The terror E.J. could hear in the man's voice was chilling. Judd leapt out of the hay loft and raced to hunker down behind the barrel that covered the hole in the barn wall.

Showtime.

E.J. had to get Buster's attention … and then submit to being mauled to death by the beast.

Death.

Big concept for such a little word. He didn't know what he thought about that, dying. What he thought about what came next. After dying. What happened then? Elijah Hamilton, doctor of veterinary medicine, did not have any idea.

But he was about to find out.

The wind blew in through the doors when he began to shove them open, sucked through the barn by the hay loft doors open up above. In the draft, it was surprisingly difficult to shove the doors outward, balanced as he was on a hoe, only putting weight on one leg. He shoved harder. One of the doors slipped out of his hand and shut itself with a loud clunking sound. Buster would hear that, wouldn't he?

E.J. shoved as hard as he could on the other door, hopping along behind it as it moved slowly forward. Where was the dog?

JUDD PERKINS HAD NEVER BEEN MORE frightened in his life. Not when he'd been in that wreck with gasoline pouring out of the truck and his seatbelt jammed. Not when he tripped and slid down Sugar Bowl Mountain to the cliff and the little tree he grabbed to keep from going over the edge started to pull out of the ground. Not when he and Bill Cochran laid down between the rails on the track while a coal train passed over.

Not even when the doctor told Mildred she had cancer and she cried all the way home and he didn't know what to say and couldn't talk at all because he was so scared.

Nothing had been as terrifying as seeing those two little girls get out of the car and start up the lane.

E.J. began to shove open the big barn doors — E.J. was giving his life for two children he barely knew. One day Judd would consider that, but not now.

As soon as E.J. began to open the doors, Judd stood up beside the big whiskey barrel and rolled it out of the way to reveal the broken boards and the hole in the side of the building. He bent down, reached out to—

He never heard a sound, not a growl, nothing. The hole was just filled suddenly with Buster's massive head, snapping, his teeth only inches from Judd's hand. Judd leapt back, stumbled, fell on his butt and scooted away from the hole while the dog clawed and snarled, breaking through the boards as it shoved its way in.

Then Judd was up and running. Flying past E.J., he slammed the barn door open crying "Buster!" and pointed back into the barn. Then he barreled full-out across the barnyard making for the back door of the house, expecting any second to feel the teeth of the huge animal buried in his flesh, the force of him pouncing on Judd's back and knocking him to the ground.

As he reached for the back door handle, he heard a sound, a voice coming from in front of the house.

"Buuusss-ter. Here, Buster! C'mere, boy."

Michelle.

He had seconds.

E.J. TURNED and saw the big dog ripping through the wall, clawing its way into the building. He rammed the boards inward, wrenching them out of the way, the old wood snapping and popping as it shattered. His massive head and shoulders exploded through the opening, his body landed in the dirt and he instantly scrambled to his feet.

E.J. pivoted, Literally. He leaned on the hoe and spun his weight around it until he was pointed at the tractor, rumbling as it idled only fifteen feet away.

He didn't even look back, just yelled.

"Buster, yo Buster. C'mere Buster, come to papa."

He leapt one step, he was aware of that. But how he made it the remaining distance was a mystery. He heard Buster behind him, maybe a step behind.

Baseball again. He dived forward to slide into home base with the winning run, straining to beat the ball in the air on the way to the catcher's mitt. With all the force he had in one leg, he leapt, hit the dirt with a bone-jarring *whump* and skidded on his belly past the inside of the big tractor's tire.

Buster growled. He had paused. Instead of leaping after E.J., he stood crouched, growling, snarling, still with that head-yanking tic moving his head from side to side.

E.J. slid to a stop.

"Buuus-ter," E.J. heard a child's voice cry from somewhere very near the barn. "Where are you, boy?'

The dog turned its massive head that way and began to rise up off his haunches.

JUDD RACED THROUGH HIS HOUSE. Grabbing his rifle off the gun rack in the den with one hand, he didn't even slow down, just plowed through the living room and out the front door and down the walk out front.

Michelle was about even with the house, running up the driveway on her way toward the barn, crying, "Buster! Buster, where are you?"

Judd slid to a stop, planted his feet wide apart, raised the rifle, put his cheek on the stock and his eye to the sight.

"Michelle, come here to me, *right now.*" He didn't turn his head toward her, just yelled, his voice a rumble of what probably sounded like rage.

And just as he feared — just as he *knew* she would — the child froze. In his peripheral vision, he saw her stop and look at him, confusion and fear stamped on her features.

"Papaw, what's wrong?"

He didn't answer, just trained the rifle on the driveway. It was a Browning A-bolt .270 hunting rifle with a Diamondback HP 3-12x42 scope. You put the crosshairs of that scope on a deer and if you knew how to work the rise on it, you could make a shot at seven hundred yards. Judd sighted on a spot as far as he could see up the driveway before the house blocked his view. He pulled in a breath and held it, his finger on the trigger. He began to apply slow pressure, squeezing it, not pulling it.

Judd would only have one shot. And regardless of all the television cop show scenes to the contrary, it was seriously difficult to deliver a fatal wound to a moving target.

⁓

E.J. COULDN'T RISE up off his flat-on-his-belly position, had only inches of clearance. But when he craned his neck to look over his shoulder at the dog behind the tractor maybe six feet away, he could see that it had risen up off its haunches and was turning toward the sound of the little girl's cry.

It was Michelle, the child with rosy cheeks, a pixie face and a turned-up nose who'd told him the last time he saw her that she could play "Twinkle, Twinkle, Little Star" on the piano.

Noooooo!

Then it came to him — maybe Mildred Perkins whispered it in his ear. In his loudest, most commanding voice, E.J. yelled, "Buster, *Hier!*"

That was "come" in German.

The dog's head snapped toward him instantly, robotically. He took a single breath, foam dripping from his mouth, the snarling growl low and deep in his throat, before he leapt at E.J.'s legs where they stuck out beyond the tractor wheel.

And a piece of that beautiful, *long* white fur caught, snagged.

E.J. turned his face away as the power take-off yanked

the dog off its feet and wound his body around and around the shaft, crushing it in seconds, mangling and mauling it until the power take-off finally jammed, and the rumble of the idling tractor and the scream of the piece of straining machinery was all E.J. could hear.

Chapter Twenty-Nine

Since hadn't nobody else noticed it, Pete hadn't said nothing about it. Might be other folks had figured it out, too, and just didn't want to say. Or might be he was the only one. It's not like stargazing was much of a hobby in the mountains, where there was only a thin slice of sky visible.

Pete had been in Arizona once, driving out across the desert at night, and he had been stunned at the expanse of stars overhead. Not because they was so bright. Most people was shocked when they got out in the open like that that the stars was big as chunks of ice, when wasn't no city lights or pollution to make them dim. But the stars above Nower County were as bright and twinkling as the ones he'd seen in the desert, it's just you couldn't see but a little bitty sliver of them because up in the mountains, you couldn't see but a little bitty sliver of sky.

It'd been after that trip to Arizona that Pete took notice of the stars he could see from his back porch at night, watched their migration across the piece of sky revealed between Little Bear Mountain and Sugar Bowl Mountain.

But after J-Day, the stars wasn't right.

At first, he thought he was imagining it, but after a while wasn't no denying reality. The stars he could see in the sky from his back porch at night were not the same stars he'd been able to see last Christmas, or the Fourth of July or Groundhog Day.

No Milky Way Galaxy, which you could sometimes see with binoculars — and he hadn't cared enough about looking to buy a telescope. No Big Dipper, Little Dipper, constellations.

The stars in the sky now ... they didn't even look real. There was just random lights. No order, no symmetry, no shapes. No big bright ones next to little-bitty pinprick ones. They was all the same size. And didn't a one of them twinkle. It was almost like they was an afterthought ... oh, wait, there's supposed to be stars in the sky — here!

Maybe he was the only one who'd noticed that, but folks was starting to talk about the weather. They *did* notice that. The last storm that had blown through Nower County had been the one the night before the Jabberwock. Folks assumed it was part of the whole Jabberwock nonsense, but Pete and some others — Malachi Tackett, for one — didn't think one was connected to the other. Folks didn't want to hear that because if the storm didn't bring it — what did? It was easier to believe that some freak of nature had brought the calamity upon them — because if it did, well, you could understand freaks of nature. Like some whale born with two heads, maybe, or an ice storm in Oklahoma in July. You might not understand what had caused it, what made it happen, but you could understand that sometimes Mother Nature just got in a bad mood and did strange things.

But a Jabberwock independent of the storm was a Jabberwock independent of all understanding. If a thing wasn't some "natural" occurrence gone inexplicably haywire, then it was — what? An *un*-natural occurrence. An event totally outside the laws and functioning of the universe. There was nowhere in the mind to put a thing like that. It was way too scary to think about, so nobody did, or if they did, they kept it to themselves.

To Pete's way of seeing it, the weather was as artificial as the stars in the sky

The skies above were always blue. Key word: always. No clouds. As in not a single cloud in two full weeks. And the temperature. This was the first couple of weeks of June *in the mountains* — the weather and the temperature had ought to be all over the map. Cool and breezy one day, rainy the next, frying pan hot a couple of days later.

Nope.

The temperature had not gotten below sixty-five degrees or above eighty-five since J-Day. He hadn't been keeping track that exactly, but he bet if he did he'd find out it was always the same temperature at noon every day. And at midnight. And every hour in between.

Dog nudged his leg, angling for a scratch behind the ears. And a treat, of course. Until he met Pete, Dog probably hadn't never in his life gotten a doggie treat. Pete had gone into Foodtown yesterday for his meager supply of groceries ... dispensed under the watchful eye of Oscar Manning, who acted like he absolutely did not want to sell anybody anything. Sell the wrong things in the wrong amounts to the wrong people was to run afoul of the Tackett clan and nobody wanted that.

The dog treats he'd bought had fallen out of the bag onto the car floorboard and Pete didn't remember them until now. So Pete went out to the car to get Dog one. He couldn't find them. Maybe he'd stuck them in the glove box. He opened it up, scratched around and his hand came to rest on the map that was now the official map of Nower County, Kentucky, so he pulled it out and shrugged his shoulders at Dog.

"They're somewhere. I am a very old man, getting older by the second, but I'll find them." He went into the house and tossed the map on the kitchen table. He'd take a look at it after he found Dog's treats, which would have to wait until after Dog's walk — which was really Pete's walk "so he could live until Christmas." Riiiiiight.

Pete fixed Dog's leash to his collar and started down his lane to the road and had just got to the parking lot when Dylan Shaw showed up. Pete didn't see all of it. He'd been looking away when the boy suddenly appeared. What caught his eye was movement, and he turned to see a kid in a dirty tee-shirt and jeans, hair wild, running dead out away from the bus shelter toward the Dollar General Store.

Just running. When Pete realized the boy was going to—

It was too late by then. The kid hit the wall of the building at a dead run, smacked into it and fell back on the ground, limp as a dishrag.

The kid's face was smashed. His nose appeared to be lying on his right cheek. He'd busted his mouth, both lips, and had likely loosened some teeth if he hadn't knocked a couple out entirely.

When Pete reached the body, he was surprised to see that the kid wasn't knocked out. He was lying on his back with his eyes *wide* open, pupils dilated so it appeared there was no color at all around them. Black holes in white eyeballs. And the eyes were jerking around the way Dog's did when he was asleep and dreaming about chasing rabbits.

Possibly, what Pete was seeing was the result of the kid's

encounter with the Jabberwock. And that was likely part of it. But Pete suspected the boy had slammed into the Jabberwock with the same ferocity and force he'd slammed into that wall — running wildly in response to some inner imperative, crossing over a rainbow bridge that didn't have nothing to do with black sparkling light and static.

Chapter Thirty

Sam hadn't been pacing while Charlie, Malachi and the Tungate brothers were gone. She definitely would have if she'd had time, might have been biting her fingernails, too. What was happening to them out there in Fearsome Hollow? Where was Abner?

But E.J. blew out of the clinic right before they left and he had not yet come back, so she had the whole operation to herself. It wasn't like it was some busy emergency room in a downtown New York hospital or anything like that, but there was a dribble of people with minor injuries or illnesses. And animals, too! This was, after all, a veterinary clinic.

When the four of them finally got back from Fearsome Hollow, they looked like death on a cracker.

All Sam got were snippets …

"… house was old, had aged a hundred years …"

"… picked the car up and moved it …"

"… Charlie yelled at it …"

"… whispers … voices …"

Before she had time to herd the four of them out of the

hallway into the breakroom so she could interrogate them, Raylynn told her there was a patient in the waiting room asking for her.

"It's Hayley Norman," Raylynn said. "She won't tell me what's wrong, won't talk to anybody but you."

Hayley Norman was the daughter of Duncan Norman, a preacher who pastored maybe a dozen tiny Pentecostal congregations in hollows all over the mountains. The biggest one in Nowhere County was Praying Hands Pentecostal Church in Wiley, a little community north of The Ridge, and it would have been crowded if more than twenty people showed up for a service. The Jabberwock had deposited Hayley in the Middle of Nowhere on J-Day temporarily unable to see or hear, and desperate to find her mother's vanished car.

Merrie spotted Charlie in the hall and raced to her mother, begging as she came, "Can I have a puppy, Mommy? Pleeeeeeease. I already picked, named him Santa Claus."

"Why …?"

"'Cause he got big claws."

Sam told Raylynn, "Tell Hayley I'll—"

That's as far as Sam got before Judd Perkins burst through the front door of the animal hospital, shirtless, his face the color of whipping cream. He ran through the waiting room into the hall, looking around frantically, found Sam, and began to babble.

"You got to see to him, he's hurt bad!"

"He who?"

"E.J." Judd grabbed Sam's hand and began dragging her outside. "Buster got him, mauled his leg bad."

"Buster?" Sam had been to Judd's house often when Mildred was sick and the big white Great Pyrenees was as gentle as a lamb.

Judd was driving E.J.'s van. Judd's two granddaughters were in the front and he had E.J. loaded up in the back.

"Buster's rabid." Then Judd amended it. "*Was* rabid. He's dead."

The two little girls sitting wide-eyed in the front seat made no effort to get out of the van.

Sam ran around to the back and climbed up into the van. E.J. was lying on the floor in the back, delirious from pain, his leg wrapped in blood-soaked, makeshift bandages with the belt tourniquet just below the knee.

"Oh, E.J.," was all Sam could say.

Judd grabbed her arm and whispered urgently in her ear. "That ain't the worst of it. He ain't vaccinated."

"What? E.J. isn't—"

"He told me, said he didn't take them shots, couldn't, said it'd take too long to explain why not but he for sure didn't take them. " The enormity of that revelation slammed into Sam's chest like a wrecking ball. Judd had to be mistaken, but she didn't have time to worry about it now.

Malachi and Judd carried E.J. into the animal hospital. They passed the waiting room where Sam saw Hayley Norman standing in the doorway staring. She instructed Raylynn to tell Hayley to come back some other day, and guided the men into the examining room on the end, the one that had a big metal tray instead of a cushioned table to lay him on. In the past couple of weeks, they'd done the best they could to convert it into an examining room for humans and it was better than nothing.

E.J. was moaning, barely conscious.

"Can you give him something for the pain?" Charlie asked.

"I don't have any painkillers. I'm not certified to administer narcotics, and even if I was, I've got better sense than to carry stuff like that around. If the druggies knew I had anything stronger than aspirin, I wouldn't make it out of my driveway before somebody knocked me over the head and stole it."

Sam turned to Judd. Malachi had left the room.

"How long has this tourniquet been on?"

"He said it was okay up to two hours and it ain't been that long. A hour, maybe. No mor'n that."

Sam shot Charlie a look that said, "I need help." Charlie merely nodded and shooed everyone else out of the room.

E.J. grabbed Sam's hand, yanked her down to him to speak because he had little air. "The girls, Michelle and Julie, they're alright, aren't they? I thought I saw them, but I'm … I might have imagined—"

"Michelle and Julie Shepperson were riding in the front seat of your van when Judd pulled in with you. Far as I could tell, there wasn't a scratch on either one of them. Now you lie back. I'm going to do what I can, which isn't much."

E.J. collapsed back onto the table. He was clearly about to go into shock and she had to work fast. She suddenly thought and looked at Charlie.

"Please tell me you don't faint at the sight of blood!"

"I don't faint at the sight of blood. I'm good to go, just tell me what to do."

Handing her a pair of scissors, she said, "Cut off the leg of his pants."

Sam quickly put on gloves, then loosened the tourniquet on E.J.'s leg — didn't release all the pressure — and the gory wound farther down his leg immediately swelled with blood. She let it bleed for a few seconds, making sure the blood flow was still good. Then she pulled the tourniquet tight again and went to work on the wound. It was a nightmare injury. She was proud of Charlie, though. She got a good look at it, the awful jagged tissue where the dog had literally bitten a hunk of flesh out of E.J.'s calf. Charlie didn't flinch.

Sam hollered over her shoulder to Raylynn, who was standing in the doorway, having handed Merrie off to Mrs. Throckmorton to go play with the kittens. "More sterile bandages, more pads." Sam had no idea how to close a wound that big. Shoot, she'd let E.J. sew up the little cut on Merrie's forehead, which was nothing more than a fading white mark now, because he was better at that kind of thing than she was. E.J. needed emergency surgery — by a trauma surgeon, a good one. And a vascular surgeon. Who knew what else — they'd have decided the specialties they needed when he was evaluated at the trauma center.

No trauma center here. No surgeons — trauma or any other kind. No emergency surgery to repair …

She remembered the oath, the one doctors were supposed to take. "First, do no harm."

She could screw something up big time if she attempted any procedure she wasn't qualified to do. What she could do — *all* she could do — was clean the wound *thoroughly*, disinfect it. Do everything she was trained to do to avoid infection. Then she would pack it to stop the bleeding, bandage it properly and … that would have to do for now. There'd be other decisions to make about what came next, but now wasn't the time to make them.

She worked fast and efficiently, with Charlie falling into the assistant role like a surgical nurse — well, except she didn't know the names of the instruments, responded to a mere, "the pincher-looking things." Once Sam had done what she could to deaden the area with Novocain and relieve some of the pain, E.J. had relaxed some, was breathing better.

"You know how to take a blood pressure?" Sam asked Charlie.

"How hard can it be? Tell me what to do."

E.J.'s pulse was rapid and thready — to be expected. His pressure was low, also to be expected. But he was not, as far as Sam could determine, in hypovolemic shock from loss of blood. She was just finishing up when Malachi appeared in the doorway as if on cue.

"I got a hospital bed outside. Where you want me to put it?" She just gawked at him. "Roscoe Tungate's wife, Miriam. She had one at the end. He went and got it."

"That room down the hall, the storage room. Clean it out so—" But Malachi was already moving.

E.J. had IV fluids for humans ... somewhere. He'd mentioned not long ago that he'd stopped using generic products in favor of veterinary specific products — said he had a bunch of the generic left over. She'd get Raylynn to find it. Sam had in her kit the proper needle for a human.

Malachi appeared at the door again, summoned by magic.

"Room's ready."

The exam table had wheels and they rolled it down the hall with E.J. aboard.

The hospital room was ... *a hospital room.* The storage room that'd been stacked high with ... everything, was now pin-neat with a hospital bed and a side table and a straight-backed chair. The floor was wet, had just been mopped. When Malachi and Judd helped E.J. from the rolling table to the bed, he cried out in pain and Malachi spoke softly into Sam's ear. "It won't be long. I've sent for pain meds. Oxycontin."

"How—?"

"Don't ask. Just know I can lay hands on all you need."

The oxy came. Sam gave E.J. two pills and would

follow that up with another two in an hour if he needed it. Watching the pain ease out of his face was glorious.

E.J. looked past Sam to Malachi standing in the doorway, gave him a thumbs up. "Good drugs, man." Malachi returned the thumbs up and E.J. closed his eyes. He was soon asleep. Sam wouldn't leave E.J.'s side until he was breathing regular and slow. Then she let Raylynn sit in the chair at his bedside, but still wouldn't leave the room.

She did go to the doorway to stand with Malachi and Charlie.

"I sent the Sheppersons home," Malachi said. Doreen had shown up at some point, and the girls wanted to see E.J. "I told them maybe tomorrow." He nodded with his chin toward the waiting room. "Judd refused to leave. He'll be here until ... said he just wanted to be close by." Malachi produced the scraps of a smile. "He did send Doreen to his house to get him a shirt, though."

Sam didn't even want to say the words. "Judd told me that—"

"E.J. isn't vaccinated," Malachi finished for her. "Told me the same thing."

"What?" Charlie was horrified. "Even *I've* been vaccinated for rabies, had to get a shot to get a visa into Guatemala."

Sam looked at her questioningly.

"Book research. How can a *veterinarian* not—?"

"You can ask him when he wakes up," Malachi said. "All I know is what Judd told me, that E.J. was adamant, said he was going to get rabies ... and die from it. That's part of the reason he did what he did."

After Malachi finished telling them the story, the three stood in the doorway, watching E.J. sleep, shocked into silence.

"I served with a lot of guys like E.J.," Malachi said

softly. "Guys who don't know they're brave until they have to be."

Charlie tacked words on the obvious.

"The clock's ticking now. If the Jabberwock doesn't … If we can't get medicine for E.J. in—" She turned to Sam. "How long? How long does he have?"

"He should have gotten the first shot within twenty-four hours, but … I'll look in the medical books E.J. got from Brian O'Conner to be sure, but … as soon as he develops symptoms, that's it. After that, there's nothing that can be done."

"How long?" Malachi asked.

"Oh, in rare cases, the virus can incubate for up to two years before—"

"How long?" Malachi said the words slowly, individually.

"A week. Ten days. Depends on how big a dose of virus … he got a big dose."

"That's it, then," Charlie said. "We've got a week to figure out how to get out of Nowhere County … or E.J. dies."

Chapter Thirty-One

When he'd arrived at the county line shortly after sunrise, Reece Tibbits had stood for a time fifty feet inside Nowhere County, looking at the shimmering mirage that hung over the highway and disappeared away from it in both directions as far as he could see. A lot of folks had real strong emotions about the Jabberwock, hated the thing that kept them all prisoner day after day. Reece didn't have any feelings about it one way or the other. It was a just a thing. How could you get your nose all out of joint about a thing? It'd be like hating a door knob or getting mad at the fender on his truck.

Reece spent half an hour throwing things through the Jabberwock. Rocks, tree branches, clods of dirt, a screwdriver and the rubber work boot he carried in the truck, the one with the hole in it. Everything passed through as if it were, indeed, a mirage. So he let down the tailgate on his pickup truck, climbed up into the bed and carefully unloaded his barrel bomb onto the wheeled pallet. It was heavy. He could have used a hand loading and unloading it even though he was as strong as a bull. But Reece didn't want to share his plan with anybody. Shoot, if word got out, he mighta had an audience out here this morning to watch the Jabberwock get blown to kingdom come.

He scooted the pallet across the asphalt toward the mirage. The rope was to ensure he didn't accidentally step too close and get sucked through the Jabberwock and deposited in the bus shelter. He had never in his life been so sick and he would just about rather die than repeat the experience.

Shoving the pallet with his foot, he fed out the fifteen feet of rope, used a mop to push it the final three feet and eased the bomb into the mirage. It sat there beside the marble he'd rolled across the asphalt, right dead center of the shimmer, but still visible and stable.

He dropped the rope onto the road, got into his truck, backed up fifty yards from the pallet and parked the pickup crossways in the middle of the road. Then he got out and lifted his rifle off the gun rack in front of the back window. Hunkering down behind his truck bed for protection from any pieces of shrapnel from the exploding oil drum, he rested the rifle barrel on the railing of the truck bed and sighted down it at his makeshift detonator.

He was about to set off a bomb to blow up … nothing.

When the dust from the pulverized asphalt settled out of the air, he was certain, convinced that's what he would see. Nothing. But a different kind of nothing. No shimmer. No mirage. *Nothing*.

His bomb would blow a hole in the Jabberwock, rip right through the thing. Then he'd go get his mother and drive her through that hole to Carlisle, where dialysis would clean the toxins out of her blood before they killed her.

He found his hand was steady when he moved his finger inside the trigger guard. Squeeze, don't pull.

Reece squeezed.

∽

IT WAS LONG past sunrise somewhere out there on the flat when Charlie McClintock staggered bleary-eyed into her mother's kitchen and found there a whole new magnitude of awful.

If it hadn't been for Merrie, she'd have given up on trying to sleep at all last night, would've gone back to the Middle of Nowhere to help Sam care for E.J. Not that Sam needed her help. Instead, Charlie had overslept after hours of tossing and turning, trying not to imagine a rabid dog mauling E.J., trying not to hear the tick, tick, tick of the clock that started its countdown when the dog attacked.

Rabies. They had seven, maybe ten days to … to what? To defeat the Jabberwock. And what that might mean she had no idea.

Coffee. Coffee made everything better.

Except it didn't this morning because as soon as she switched on the coffeemaker, she turned toward the blackboard on the wall … and everything went south after that.

The next thing she knew, she was sitting on the floor with her legs folded beneath her.

Nothing registered in between. No decision to sit down. No "Okay, legs, let's bend at the knee now so …" Nothing like that. She hadn't *decided* to sit down. Her legs had collapsed out from under her.

They'd mutinied, declined to hold her upright — not now, not with yet another *something unexplainable* displayed for her viewing enjoyment right here in her own kitchen.

No.

No, no, no, no.

Reality refused to budge.

And so she stared at the words chalked in bold strokes in the center of the blackboard.

Not the words her mother had written, words Charlie could not, would not erase. Not "get bird seed" in her mother's precise cursive in the top left corner.

Other words, big and bold — three of them.

Where are you?

She recognized the handwriting. *It was Stuart's.*

How could it possibly be …?

She ground her teeth together. Stuart wanted to know where she was — *riiiiiight*. Like he cared where she was! Leaping to her feet, she rushed to the blackboard, picked up the piece of chalk and wrote beneath the three words.

"I'm trapped. It won't let me go!"

She stared at what she'd written, wondering why her mind had burped out those particular words. She started to write more, describe that she was right here *where Stuart had left her.* But she didn't. She looked at the chalkboard through a blur of tears. Of course, *Charlie had written the words* — last night when she'd come home so tired and distraught she didn't even remember doing it. Clearly, her exhaustion had weakened her more than she knew, and she flushed in shame at her pathetic effort to make it seem like Stuart gave a rip what happened to her and Merrie. The man had made it abundantly clear that he did not!

SHE HOLDS the credit card statement in trembling fingers as she dials the number the information operator had given her.

"Marriott, Oahu."

Not Seattle, working out the details of some big corporate merger. Hawaii.

The man's voice in her ear is speaking and she struggles to attach meaning to the words.

"... help you?"

"Would you please connect me to the room of ... Stuart McClintock."

There is a pause.

"I'm sorry, ma'am, but that room has a call block."

"Call block?"

"That's when guests request they not be disturbed by incoming calls."

"Guests? As in more than one?"

"I can't give out guest information over the phone—"

"I just want to know if—"

"I'm sorry. Is there anything else I can help you with?"

Charlie is desperate. She has to know.

"Do you have children?"

"I beg your pardon?"

"Children. Little kids. Do you have any?"

"Ma'am ... I think perhaps you need to speak to the manager."

"Because if you have kids, I can tell them a secret every child in North America would like to know."

There's a pause. Maybe she's hooked him.

"I can tell them what the final book in the Alphabet Gang series is about."

"The Alphabet Gang?"

Recognition and curiosity.

"I'm the author. C.R.R. Underhill — stands for Charlene Renee Ryan — and the Underhill part is from The Lord of the Rings *... the inn in Bree." She is babbling and she grabs hold of her torrent of words. "The last book in* The Alphabet Gang *series is about an invisible dragon. I'll tell you the dragon's name" — which she hasn't decided yet — "if you'll just put me through to Stuart—"*

"My kids would kill to know ... but I can't connect you—"

"Please! It's an emergency. A ... medical emergency!"

"—because it wouldn't do any good. I saw them leave early this

morning with the guide from the Palms Sight-Seeing service. Those personalized tours last all day."

"Them?"

"Mr. and Mrs. McClintock. They were holding hands. So ... what's the dragon's—"

Charlie hangs up.

HER PATHETIC EFFORT TO comfort herself with Stuart's caring was just that. Pathetic. Pitiful.

Grabbing the eraser out of the tray, she applied it with force to the blackboard. Careful not to erase "get bird seed," she wiped out everything else, wiped over and over until every speck of chalk was gone.

Chucking the eraser back into the tray, she didn't pour herself a cup of coffee from the now-brewed pot. Sam would have coffee at the clinic in the Middle of Nowhere.

SAM SPENT the night in E.J.'s room, called and arranged for Rusty to stay overnight with a friend.

"Is E.J. going to be alright, Mom?" he'd asked. Rusty liked E.J. Everybody did. The boy had only been three years old when she and E.J. had dated for a month or two before agreeing their relationship had "all the pizazz of kissing your sister." After that, they were great friends.

"He's fine right now."

"I hear a 'but' in there. What is it?"

Sam tried hard not to lie to her son.

"E.J. wasn't vaccinated against rabies. So ..."

"He's going to get rabies?" Rusty was horrified.

"No, not necessarily."

"But you don't have the medicine he needs, do you? And if the Jabberwock …?"

Yeah, if the Jabberwock …

Sam had managed to persuade Raylynn to go home last night by telling her that she would need her to stay with E.J. tomorrow, and Raylynn needed to get some sleep. The girl showed up right after sunrise.

"Is he going to …?" she'd asked and the fear and concern on her face was touching. It was amazing to Sam that E.J. didn't know how the teenager felt about him. But maybe he did, just pretended to be clueless because that was less embarrassing than telling a smitten seventeen-year-old that they were not destined to be star-crossed lovers.

"We're all doing the best we can," Sam said, which wasn't an answer but it was all her tired mind could come up with.

Sam hung around the clinic all morning, was reluctant to leave the building … not yet. Judd was still there, too, had stayed the night, wouldn't leave until he had a chance to talk to E.J. She and Judd talked for a long time and his description of what had happened was the stuff of nightmares.

Sam wanted to have an equally long and detailed conversation about what'd happened in Fearsome Hollow the day before when Charlie, Malachi and the Tungates went looking for Abner. But she'd have to wait. Malachi had left in the wee hours of the morning, used E.J.'s van to go home and "gather up a few things." He had decided he would "camp out" in E.J.'s apartment in the second floor of the clinic … just to be around if anybody needed him.

His eyes hadn't looked haunted when he'd been dashing around, fixing things for E.J. In an ironic twist, the

Jabberwock was slowly dragging Malachi back from the brink of darkness.

About midmorning, Malachi came in the back door of the clinic at the same time Liam Montgomery came in the front. Liam looked around the waiting room, then asked Sam, "Have you seen Reece Tibbits?"

"No, why?"

"I thought he'd be here — out front, I mean."

"You mean ... took a ride on the Jabberwock?" Malachi asked.

"I think he tried to get out. Leave. I was sure I'd find him here, puking his guts up. So if he's not here, where did he go?"

"He tried to *get out*, you mean leave the county?" Malachi said.

"That's what it sounds like," Liam said. "Tried to blast his way out. Lonnie Monroe called in and said he'd heard an explosion right after sunrise, but he didn't go out to see what it was until a little while ago. Found Reece's truck parked crossways in the middle of Lexington Road on the county line with his rifle lying beside it, like he dropped it. I haven't been out there yet, thought I'd stop by here first and talk to Reece. Lonnie said it looked like Reece blew a hole in the road."

"So where's Reece?" Sam asked.

"That's what I'm trying to find out," Liam said.

Chapter Thirty-Two

A roaring boom hammered Reece Tibbits's ears and an invisible hand of concussion slapped the side of his truck, shoving it sideways and knocking him backwards off his feet. The rifle flew out of his hand, clattering down on the asphalt beside him.

He lay where he'd fallen, his ears throbbing. *Whahm, whahm, whahm.* The roar reminded him of the sound he'd heard when he and his mother had been driving to her dialysis appointment in Carlisle on J-Day and crossed the county line.

Black, sparkling light had brightened/darkened the world, a sound like static filled his ears and the next thing he knew he was desperately sick in the Middle of Nowhere. His mother suffered only a nosebleed, and Sam Sheridan soon got that under control, then he watched for hours as his mother pitched in to help the others who had "ridden the Jabberwock" — while he remained too sick even to sit up.

Reece didn't wake up in the Middle of Nowhere this time. He didn't lose awareness at all because he was still in the right world where the universe functioned predictably. Getting slowly to his feet, he gaped at the plume of dirt and dust and pulverized asphalt that rose more than a hundred feet in the air, all that remained of an area of roadway big as his garage that had exploded when the bomb went off. He hadn't really considered the size of the hole the explosion would blow in the road from the force directed *downward*. The *upward* force was all that had interested Reece. Upward into the Jabberwock.

He walked toward the plume still settling out of the air, so thick you couldn't see anything. He couldn't tell yet if he had done what he'd intended to do.

Then he saw the man standing beside his car on the *other side of the Jabberwock*. Only there was no shimmering mirage between the two of them. Reece merely stood there, gawking. The look of shocked surprise on his own face likely matched the expression on the face of the man standing beside his open car door, gaping at the falling debris and the hole in the road.

The man was big, muscled, dressed in a suit that he wore like he slept in one, immaculate, red power tie. He was black, with his hair cut close to his head, and he reminded Reece of some movie star, but Reece couldn't place who it was. The man had obviously been driving down the road when the asphalt exploded in front of him.

Reece almost giggled.

Incoming round!

Now *that'd* be a surprise — an exploding road.

The guy on the other side was driving a red Lexus — not gaudy red, of course. A subdued, dignified red. Had Fayette County plates, looked like an airport rental. Bet it didn't have 150 miles on it, just the distance this guy had driven here from Lexington, probably still smelled new inside.

Then his thoughts stopped bouncing off the insides of his skull and stilled, and that's when he realized *he had done it*. Reece had blown a hole in the Jabberwock, had punched right though it to the other side. That dude standing beside his car out there on the road could get back behind the wheel and drive right on into Nowhere County — well, could have if there hadn't been a hole in the road in front of him. That'd be a challenge, which, admittedly, Reece hadn't given enough consideration. He knew there'd be damage to the road, but *this* … Well, the guy'd just have to take that shiny new car off-road, that's all. The tangle of weeds and bushes, briars, thistles and wildflowers — asters, bluebells, monkey flowers and lilies — were like to scratch up that pretty red paint job when he plowed through them, but there was plenty of room on the roadside to drive around the hole.

Mama!

Mama wasn't going to die after all. He'd saved her. He needed to go *now* and get her, take her to Carlisle for dialysis. She'd be her old self again by suppertime.

Reece grinned at the surprised man, who'd made no move to do anything except get out of his car and stand there behind the door. Reece reached up his hand to wave, and then the smile on Reece's face drained away.

Up above the shrinking plume of dust and falling debris was the shimmering surface of a mirage. It was settling back to earth with the dust.

It didn't look like it had looked before, though. It had a hole in it, but not a jagged one like Reece had blown in the road. The hole was perfectly round, probably twenty feet in diameter, big enough to drive a tank through … except it was shrinking. Like the aperture on a camera, it was closing, still round but getting smaller and smaller.

The hole in the shimmer floating down out of the sky

atop the dust cloud wasn't flat, though. It was *protruding*, like an outie navel, becoming more and more pointed.

Aimed at Reece.

Then the shimmer began to move *toward Reece*. Faster and faster, with the hole closing. It took him a second to be afraid. By then, the shimmer had formed a cone shape and was flying at him like an arrow.

Suddenly more than frightened, Reece was terrified. He turned and bolted down the road away from the shimmer — looking over his shoulder, watching the cone of mirage fly through the air at him. He tripped over his own feet, stumbled and fell forward, peeling the skin off the palms of his hands and ripping the knees out of his coveralls when he hit the road — like he did when he was a kid and fell on the sidewalk.

And Mama would kiss it when he went into the house crying. She'd make it well.

Reece flipped over onto his back and the cone was hovering over him, not six feet away. He looked up through the open cone, *into* the shimmer. *Into the Jabberwock.*

He saw them then, saw their faces.

And Reece Tibbits began to scream.

STUART MCCLINTOCK STARED in gap-jawed amazement at the man standing on the other side of the gigantic hole in the asphalt where dust and debris were still sifting down out of the sky. The man wore a tee shirt beneath bib over-alls and had a streak of white like a lightning bolt in his black hair.

He looked like he was about to wave at Stuart. Instead, he turned and ran away, tripped and face-planted on the road. When he rolled over, he began to scream, an other-worldly shriek that—

Cut off suddenly. Then it was silent. There was no sound at all. There was no man, either. He had *vanished*.

THE END

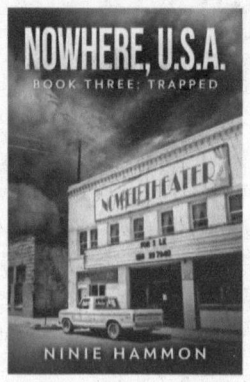

A Note from the Author

Thank you for reading *Mad Dog*.

If you enjoyed this book, you please consider writing a review on your favorite bookselling site so other readers might enjoy it too. Just a couple of sentences would mean a lot to me.

Thank you!

Ninie Hammon

About the Author

Ninie Hammon (rhymes with shiny, not skinny) grew up in Muleshoe, Texas, got a BA in English and theatre from Texas Tech University and snagged a job as a newspaper reporter. She didn't know a thing about journalism, but her editor said if she could write he could teach her the rest of it and if she couldn't write the rest of it didn't matter. She hung in there for a 25-year career as a journalist. As soon as she figured out that making up the facts was a whole lot more fun than reporting them, she turned to fiction and never looked back.

Ninie now writes suspense--every flavor except pistachio: psychological suspense, inspirational suspense, suspense thrillers, paranormal suspense, suspense mysteries.

In every book she keeps this promise to her Loyal Reader: "I will tell you a story in a distinctive voice you'll always recognize, about people as ordinary as you are--people who have been slammed by something they didn't sign on for, and now they must fight for their lives. Then smack in the middle of their everyday worlds, those people encounter the unexplainable--and it's always the game-changer."

Also By Ninie Hammon

Cornbread Mafia

Fire In The Hole

Blown' Up A Storm

Ridin' For A Fall

Nowhere, USA

The Jabberwock

Mad Dog

Trapped

The Hanging Judge

The Witch of Gideon

Blown Away

Nowhere People

Through The Canvas Series

Black Water

Red Web

Gold Promise

Blue Tears

The Taken Saga

The Taken

The Changed

The Hidden

The Saved

The Unexplainable Collection

Five Days in May

Black Sunshine

The Based on True Stories Collection

Home Grown

Sudan

When Butterflies Cry

The Knowing Series

The Knowing

The Deceiving

The Reckoning

The Fault

Stand-alone Psychological Thrillers

The Memory Closet

The Last Safe Place